I0631011

"A girl needs a man with some fire!" drawled the gorgeous blonde.

And dough, Hugh North added silently as the little minx snuggled up closer.

North was masquerading as "Yahoo" Gregory, the fabulously wealthy uranium king. He was playing his part to the hilt— fancy shirt, twenty-gallon hat, bourbon by the bottle and money to burn.

Gregory had been secretly invited to Bermuda to join a dangerous international conspiracy. Fortunately, Colonel Hugh North, expert G-2 agent, had a striking resemblance to Yahoo, so the State Department ordered a switch.

So far so good. No one—not even the clinging blond fortune hunter—had any reason to be suspicious. But North was walking a knife edge. One false move and he would turn up as a *corpse!*

The plot of **THE MULTIMILLION-DOLLAR MURDERS** is based in part on a much earlier novel by the author, **The Castle Island Case.**

OTHER BOOKS BY F. VAN WYCK MASON

F. VAN WYCK MASON

THE

Multi-million-dollar Murders

WILDSIDE PRESS

An earlier version of *The Multimillion-Dollar Murders* was published in 1937, under the title *The Castle Island Case,* by Reynal & Hitchcock, Inc.

Copyright, 1937, ©, 1960, by F. van Wyck Mason. All rights reserved.

Cast of Characters

1.

JUDY FORTHIER kept her eyes pinned on her dressing-table mirror. The reflection of the person who stood behind her smiled gently, with infinite evil.

Judy's voice was firm, no matter that she knew she was doomed. "You won't get away with this, you know."

The other's voice was little more than a whisper. "Oh, yes I will. I'm quite sure I will. Nobody could possibly suspect me, any more than they could imagine that you're who you really are."

The Forthier girl pushed aside the pack of playing cards that so incongruously occupied the center of the dressing table. Her tapered fingers toyed with a tiny pair of manicure scissors.

"And don't try anything foolish with those things," the hushed voice advised.

Judy looked at the gleaming stiletto that shone in the vanity mirror. "I could scream," she said, and was proud of the fact that her voice did not tremble.

"And who would hear you?" the other mocked. "You could scream your pretty head off, and nobody at that party would miss a swallow of a drink or a step of the cha-cha. No, my sweet, I'm afraid you haven't a chance."

Judy slowly, slowly doubled her feet under the dressing-table bench. She knew now that she had made a mistake, several bad mistakes. She had expected something like this but from another direction; she had made sure that the one she had so mistakenly feared was occupied when she had stolen away from the noisy party to come here. It was a joke, a ghastly joke, that she had even told the really dangerous one, this person she had never feared, that she was going to her room with a headache.

. They had told her that a person in her work seldom was given a chance to rectify a stupid mistake, and they had been right.

Her only chance now lay in somehow evading that poised stiletto, knocking aside the swift-slashing stab, and making the door across the room. There was a chance in spite of the fact that the killer was so much stronger, so hair-triggered of mind and muscle.

"You don't have to kill me, you know," she said conversationally. "I'll leave Freebooter's Hall. I promise I'll go away first thing in the morning."

The reflection smiled again. "Poor girl. I'd say yes to that in a minute if you didn't know quite so much."

"But I promise you—" And Judy Forthier flung herself upward, striking at the knife with a down-sweeping, chopping backward blow.

. The little throw rug beneath her feet betrayed her. It skidded on the terrazzo floor, and as she felt her footing fail, Judy Forthier knew she would be dead within seconds.

She half turned, reaching for the knife her unbalanced blow had missed, and for a moment she saw terror and hate in the killer's eyes. Then the stiletto came up and pierced Judy Forthier's young breast, and she fell forward, coughing, as the lights dimmed and the life went out of her.

[2]

Colonel Hugh North, Army Intelligence, looked down from the window of the big cabin plane to watch the lights of ·Idlewild Airport revolve slowly and then recede into the night behind him.

He relaxed in his seat, grinned at the young man sitting across the compartment—more of a drawing room than a plane cabin, actually—and said: "I don't want to be a Texas oil millionaire, Kenny; I just want to travel like one—like this."

His aide, Lieutenant Kenny Trotter, nodded approvingly. "I always said that if I stuck with you long enough you'd come up with an assignment that wouldn't be all fleas and heat and Malay cutthroats," he said. "A couple of more jobs like this and I may consider making this a permanent connection."

Which, to the outsider, might seem a peculiar way for a junior officer to speak to his superior, but that was the way Kenny Trotter spoke to Hugh North—when, and only when, the two were alone in their mutually respectful camaraderie. And alone they were, thousands of feet over the Atlantic in one of the most luxurious private planes ever built, heading for Bermuda, Plunder Island, detailed to investigate suspected murder, hot on the strong scent of international intrigue.

Forward in the control cabin were pilot and co-pilot; aft in the galley was a steward; but the two G-2 agents, colonel and aide, were secure in their isolation. This plane had been built to specifications that insured occupants of the lounge cabin complete privacy. The owner of the aircraft, William ("Wildcat Bill") Allenby, had demanded that it be soundproof, intrusion-proof, so that he could swing his oil deals without fear of the machinations of the cleverest industrial spy.

It was seldom that Wildcat Bill lent his flying hideaway to anyone. Before this, those few men who had used the plane had been brothers in the fabulous oil empire, other tycoons who had wanted to transact deals so gigantic and supersecret that they had refused to trust ordinary precautions —or who had wanted a week-end sanctuary that was raid-proof against an irate wife's possible interference.

Hugh North and Kenny Trotter were the first nonmillionaires to be lent the plane, and they were using it now because Wildcat Bill Allenby was a patriot and a hater of wealthy snobs. When certain high government officials had hinted to Allenby the urgencies of the case of Wesley Grafton, Townley Ward, and Judy Forthier, the oilman had been prompt to go down the line with G-2. He had thrust his plane upon Army Intelligence, no questions asked, and as a result, Colonel North and Lieutenant Trotter were traveling to Bermuda in a style to which, considering the Army pay each received, it behooved neither to become accustomed.

Both men were in civilian clothes, if Hugh's gaudy costume could be called such. The G-2 colonel wore a pair of tight fawn-colored pants, shin-length boots heavily embroidered in gold thread, a double-breasted and embroidered silk shirt, complete with massive neck cord medallion instead of a necktie, and a twenty-gallon hat that had cost G-2 a hundred and sixty-five dollars to furnish. He was, in the words of his irreverent aide, a cross between Roy Rogers gone berserk and the ghost of Buffalo Bill Cody.

Kenny Trotter, in fact, had had trouble looking at his superior without doubling over in helpless laughter when he had first rehearsed his role of secretary to the man Hugh North was supposed to be, Ogden Forrest ("Yahoo") Gregory.

"Oh, God," he had moaned during one of these seizures, "I've got to manage somehow to get color pictures of you in that get-up—they'll be my convincer when I ask you to okay my captaincy, or else."

"Laugh, damn you," North had retorted between clenched teeth. "I hope our next assignment has you dressing like a beatnik. Complete with beard."

"That shirt," Kenny gurgled. "Them pants."

"And another thing," Hugh warned. "You make one pass at a girl on Plunder Island and I'll say you've got a wife and four kids back home. I mean it."

Kenny sobered exaggeratedly. "Yes, Mr. Gregory. Very good, Mr. Gregory."

"And don't talk like a stage butler, for God's sake," Colonel North had added. "It'll require some effort on your part to hit a medium between the servile and your natural insufferability."

"And Yahoo Gregory would never use a word like insufferability," Trotter warned. "You'd better watch yourself, *mon colonel.*"

"Never mind about me. You just study that dossier you've got on this gang we're going to meet. One foul-up and you'll hear Yahoo Gregory blow the whistle on his good-looking young secretary, wrecking all chances for romance."

"Ah yes, the dossier," Kenny said, and picked up that thick sheaf of papers with a sigh. He had studied the facts contained in this file hours upon end, as had Hugh North, until now, as the plane boomed through the night toward Bermuda, the G-2 colonel and his aide were as confident as they were about anything connected with this job that they could pose successfully as Yahoo Gregory, latest of the uranium multimillionaires, and his private secretary.

Still, as was his habit when he was getting ready to step into a new case in a new role, North mentally recited the facts at hand to make sure he had them letter-perfect. Kenny Trotter, recognizing the look on his colonel's face, lapsed into silence.

North was harking back to the day he had walked into G-2 headquarters in the Pentagon at the end of a fast plane trip from the Orient in response to an urgent command, the day he had been given this dossier.

A conference was in session when Hugh arrived, a parley headed by North's chief, the General, and attended by not only top men of G-2, but—and North had been surprised at this—leading figures of the State Department's Counterintelligence Division.

"Have a chair, Colonel," the General had barked. "You know Rogers of Counterintelligence, I believe." North and the tall, taciturn Rogers had shaken hands, and then the General had introduced Hugh to those of the others he had not met previously.

"Okay, let's get down to business," the General said when the pleasantries were finished. "How'd you like to be a multimillionaire for a while, Hugh?"

The General seldom joked on occasions like this. North,

therefore, knew immediately that he was going to act the part of a multimillionaire for a while. It was that simple.

"Might enjoy it, sir," he had replied, smiling.

"After the stinking jobs you've had lately, I think you do deserve this break," the General had grinned. "And this is really a break." He leaned back in his chair and shot another question. "What do you know about Yahoo Gregory?"

Hugh shrugged. "About what everybody knows, I suppose, sir. Made the richest uranium strike ever known about four years ago. Was nothing before that—he's splashed it high, wide, and handsome ever since. Likes women in wholesale lots. Gets his picture in the paper every other day or so. Sort of a ridiculous gent, if you ask me, sir."

"Ever met him?"

"No, sir. We don't travel in the same circles."

The General had leaned back in his chair, grinning, before he had nodded to an aide standing beside the door. The light colonel had left the room and had returned in a moment with the most flamboyant man Hugh North had ever seen.

It was, without doubt, Ogden Forrest ("Yahoo") Gregory in all his glory. That day he wore a pure white outfit with white boots, the whole tastefully decorated in purple that had come close to matching his choleric complexion. It was incredible to Hugh that a man could dress like that as anything but a gag, but it was no gag with Yahoo; the uranium millionaire had let that be known with his first words.

"Look at 'em and blink," he had roared at North as the G-2 colonel had stared. "Ever seen clothes like these outside the movies, podner? Bet you ain't—or in the movies, either. Put 'er there."

Still half expecting this conference to break up in hoots of laughter, North had extended his hand to be claimed by the beartrap grip of Yahoo. The uranium king had leaned back in the midst of that bone-crushing exchange and had beamed at North.

"Damn if you *don't* look some'n like me," he had boomed. "A little peaked in your colorin', mebbe, but you'll pass, you'll pass."

And Hugh, when his eyes managed to look past the blazing spectacle of those clothes, had found to his amazement that he *did* resemble Yahoo in a general way. The uranium man was not as tall nor were his shoulders as broad; he was thicker in the middle than North, but the eyes, the chin, even the faint slant of the once-fractured nose, were almost identical.

"Go get 'em, Colonel," Yahoo had roared. "Anything you do to that gang is okay with me. Just don't sign no papers in my name for over fifty million bucks is all I ask. It'd make me cut down on my bourbon 'n' branchwater fer at least a week."

With which, emitting howls of laughter at his own wit, the uranium tycoon had been led out of the conference room, and that was the last that Hugh North had seen of Yahoo Gregory.

"Think you can play the part?" Hugh's chief had asked in the silence that had followed Yahoo's departure.

North nodded. It would be a cinch to imitate such a hell-roarer as Yahoo; it was the quiet man with the subtle mannerisms who required exhaustive study and rehearsal. "Yes, sir, I think so," the colonel had said.

The General slapped the conference table in front of him. "Good. Knew you could. You'll have to put some beefsteak red in your face and—but you know better than I how to do the job, Hugh."

"One thing," Colonel North cautioned. "This man has been photographed by about everybody with a camera. Won't the people I'm supposed to convince—"

"He's been photographed plenty, God knows," the General broke in, "but always with that sombrero on, shading half his face. He always wears a wide-brimmed hat—always. Supposed to be bald and touchy about it. Won't wear a toupee; just keeps his hat on all the time and to hell with the proprieties. At least that's the story. He might sleep in that sombrero, for all we know. None of the crowd you're going to convince has ever met Yahoo."

"Now, we're not absolutely sure Ward hasn't," the head of the State Department delegation, Rogers, put in. "We do know Ward has tried to see Gregory plenty of times, but so far as Yahoo remembers he never actually met Ward—at least not while he was sober."

"That's Townley Ward," Hugh's chief had supplied. "Know him?"

"Know of him, of course," Hugh had answered. As who didn't? Born to millions, of an old established society family, Townley Ward had established a name in a dozen "right" fields—sports cars, polo, college football, and, more recently, in finance where, despite the fact that he was young and handsome and still a party-goer, he had masterminded some business coups that had made his elders blink.

And what had Townley Ward to do with this emergency meeting in the Pentagon? What had Yahoo Gregory? What was this all about, anyway?

As if in answer to Hugh North's unspoken questions, the General hunched over the conference table and filled him in.

Two days previously, Yahoo Gregory had been approached by a devious, hush-hush channel with word that Wesley C. Grafton, a financier whose bankroll and family background eclipsed in many ways his business ethics, was extremely desirous of seeing him and talking to him. There was a deal on the fire in which Grafton was sure Yahoo would be interested, a deal involving millions, of course, but more than that, Power, something new to the recently emerged uranium king.

Grafton was in Bermuda, occupying his sprawling estate on Plunder Island, and would Yahoo Gregory consider coming to the island to discuss certain matters that might be to his interests, moneywise and in the fascinating field of international intrigue? Oh, of course the thing had not been put so baldly, but even Yahoo had known that more than crass dollars were involved; he had plenty of those and Grafton was trolling the bait of a new, exciting, stimulating offer, a chance at the strings that controlled world politics.

"In spite of the loud noise he makes and the clothes he wears," the General had told North, "Mr. Gregory is a man of principle and patriotism. He smelled something foul about the deal. He contacted the State Department—also through a devious, hush-hush channel."

Rogers had taken it from there. "We already had our eye on Grafton," he said. "He's been involved in some deals that came pretty close to the line, but so far he hasn't stepped over."

"What kind of line?" Hugh had asked.

Rogers had lifted his shoulders. "Such things as backing people and parties in other countries who were opposed to the people and parties we wanted to stay in office," he explained. "Financing a revolution where it might have been Washington's fervent wish to have no revolution. He's been very clever about it. So far we haven't been able to nail him on one single count, but according to what we hear, he might be getting either cocky or anxious and this might be the time he'll slip up and we can grab him."

Hugh had swung back to his General. "Frankly, I don't get it, sir," he had admitted. "Isn't this strictly a job for State? How does G-2 come into the picture?"

"By a technical loophole, if you want to call it that," the chief had grinned. "Yahoo's uranium finds its way into Army uses. We like to look out for our uranium producers, you see."

"And," Rogers had put in, "C.I.D. has pulled a blank. We admit it."

"Add to that the fact that you're almost Yahoo's twin and you can see why we moved in," the General had continued. "With State's complete cooperation, of course."

"At State's request, as a matter of fact," Rogers said wryly. "We got off on the wrong foot in this case—or at least we suppose we did. Our agent—but I'll let the General supply the details."

"Okay," Hugh's superior said in his growling voice. "Here it is: Your dossiers will dot the *i*'s for you, but this is the general situation. Grafton is planning some big coup. He's got Townley Ward with him at Plunder Island; he thinks Yahoo Gregory is coming down. The deal smells like a manufactured revolution—since Castro, those little banana republics are sitting ducks for agitators. If that's it and the revolution succeeds, the ins will be tossed out and the rebels will be tied to the syndicate that finances them. Swell chance for Grafton and Company to clean up with monopolies and so forth. Which might be all right except that in these days of global defense we want to make sure the Reds don't get a foothold in our back yard. These financiers playing with international politics too often don't investigate their stooges carefully enough. The Commies have slid into office before when big money played with revolution—we don't want it to happen again."

"So I'm to pose as Gregory and find out what's going on at Grafton's island?" North had asked.

"There's a little more to it than that," the General had frowned. He turned to Rogers. "Suppose you tell him about Judy Forthier."

Rogers was lean, dark, soft-spoken. Hugh had worked with him before and had an enormous respect for the man's ability.

"We planted an agent in Grafton's entourage," the State Department official explained. "A girl, Judy Forthier. Great charm plus plenty· of savvy and courage. She was secretary to Grafton's wife, first, and then to Grafton, shortly after the Graftons moved to Plunder Island for the winter. She sent in her reports okay—direct, no drop—but there wasn't much to tell. The deal was just beginning to jell when there came the news that Judy had had an accident. Seems she went swimming at night and drowned. Or at least disappeared—the body was never recovered."

Hugh North looked from Rogers to his General. Both men were grim. "You think she was murdered?" the colonel asked.

It was Rogers who replied. "Obvious deduction," he said, "but there are certain arguments against it. We don't *think* Grafton's a killer; he's a wealthy blueblood who might play dangerous games in finance and politics but who hardly could be expected to murder a woman when he discovered she was a government agent. Same thing with Townley Ward. The deal, I repeat, was just beginning to take form, according to Judy's last reports; Grafton could have simply kicked Judy out if he found out who she was—why kill her? It *could* have been an accident—a shark, barracuda, cramps."

"One question," Hugh said thoughtfully. "Did Miss Forthier play the agent game all the way?"

Rogers shrugged again. "She had remarkable success even though she was not especially brilliant mentally," he said quietly. "Let's leave it at that. We don't question our women agents' methods too closely when they come up with what we want."

North nodded understandingly. Judy Forthier might have played it all the way, in which case there could always be a chance of a heart interest in a killing.

"We want you to find out what happened to Judy, Colonel," Rogers was saying, "along with what's cooking on Plunder Island. No need to tell you how we all feel about our agents being killed—it happens from time to time, but the killer always pays."

Hugh nodded. "Has this been cleared with British Intelligence?" he asked. "Or don't you want them bothered?"

The General and Rogers exchanged glances. "I'm sure British Intelligence has plenty to occupy them without our bringing them into this case," the General said finally. "Of course, they already might be hip-deep in this thing. There might even be a British agent at Plunder Island, although I understand Miss Forthier couldn't spot any. You see, Colonel, it might be that the country involved in Grafton's little deal is one where the British might like to see a change of government, too. They wouldn't want the Commies in there, of course, but suppose the present regime was pro-American to the exclusion of British trade interests? Get the idea?"

Hugh nodded. "And nobody's sure what country Grafton's aiming at?"

"Hell, no," the General had said explosively. "If we knew that we'd work from that end to make sure Grafton's plans gang agley. That's for you to find out and tell us at the earliest possible moment."

He had reached for thick sheaves of papers. "Here's your dope on the man you're going to be—Yahoo Gregory," he said, shoving the file across the table toward North. "Here's a guest list—or the best available—of the crowd at Freebooter's Hall, Grafton's place on Plunder Island. We've borrowed a pretty incredible plane for your use. Your aide, Lieutenant Trotter, will be your secretary. Anything else, Rogers?"

"One thing," the Counterintelligence man had said slowly. "When Judy's disappearance made the newspapers, up popped a woman claiming to be her sister. She calls herself Patricia Forthier, and she flew out to Bermuda before we could get any kind of a line on her. Judy's file shows no sister. This other woman may be a phoney so watch her."

North had gathered up his bulky files and stood up. Unless those dossiers contained a lot of improbable details he would have to play this mostly by ear. Well, he had done that often enough, and he'd been lucky enough to pick the right tune more often than not. Of course he had never before posed as a loud-mouthed uranium prospector who had struck it rich, but that promised to be a welcome relief from some of the other roles he had had to play in the past. In fact it should be a ball.

If the Commies had not disposed of Judy Forthier. *If* they were not on Plunder Island, waiting to see what other agent might appear to be disposed of.

"Looks like we're coming in, *mon colonel*," Kenny Trotter said from across the lounge cabin. "Ah, for the good old days when we could have taken the *Monarch of Bermuda* or some other plush liner instead of skipping over in a couple of hours. Shipboard would give us a chance to meet some wimmen, have some fun. This way—"

"Complaining already?" North broke in. "Remember Sanga Sanga? Remember Seoul and a couple of other places like that? And this is bad?"

"This," said Lieutenant Kenny Trotter firmly, "is wonderful. Forget I opened my big mouth."

[3]

The big cabin plane circled the airport at St. George in a lazy orbit, then took the tower's instructions to come in. Even Trotter, a hot jet pilot himself, had to admit that Wildcat Allenby, the millionaire who had lent G-2 this ship, hired able pilots; the luxurious aircraft touched down with scarcely a jar.

The plane taxied up to the private airplane apron, and its twin turbo-jet engines ceased their powerful, throaty grumble. The steward threw open the wide doorway and let down the mechanical landing stage the plane carried. Colonel North emerged from the plane and descended to the concrete apron, Kenny Trotter behind him, carrying the badge of the private secretary, the cowhide attaché case.

The hour was nine o'clock, Bermuda time, and the airport was relatively quiet. On the runways where the commercial planes landed and took off there was a stir of activity as floodlights illumined one of the huge transports that appeared ready to depart. On the leased U.S. airbase adjoining, all was dark except for the glimmer of subdued lights in the ready room, the bullpen, the quarters where S.A.C. and interceptor pilots kept vigil against the black day or night when the order to *Scramble!* might be for real.

Hugh looked about, feet planted wide, huge hat shoved back on his forehead, his hands on his hips. "Where in hell is everybody?" he roared in a voice calculated to carry over the entire airport. "Mean t'say they invited me down here and then forgot to meet me? Tell 'em to crank up the engines again, Kenny-boy. Nobody gives Yahoo Gregory the brush-off like this."

Hugh North had played many roles but never before had he tried one that was such a strain on his vocal chords. His study of Yahoo's case history plus an intensified audience of tapes that carried Gregory's booming voice had showed him that Yahoo never spoke in a tone lower than a bellow. The uranium millionaire was an extrovert to end all extroverts; apparently his millions had given him the chance to make up for all those lonely years of prospecting by taking the center of every stage he stepped upon, loudly demanding attention.

Now, as he stood beside the big plane that had carried him from Idlewild, North wore the make-up needed to transform his sun-bronzed complexion into the beefy, high-blood-pressurized countenance of Yahoo Gregory. The colonel protruded his stomach a fraction to give himself the watermelon that Yahoo was developing; the G-2 agent walked with the slightest hint of a limp in his left leg because, twenty years before, the real Yahoo had fallen into a gulch with only a mule to tend him and had set his own broken leg, admirably for an amateur but not quite well enough to escape the limp.

"Where they at?" North howled. "You sure you got the date right for thisyere meetin', Kenny-boy?"

"Yes, Mr. Gregory," Trotter said in a Harvardian voice. "It's all in the transcript of your telephone conversation with Mr. Grafton. Nine o'clock, Bermuda time, on the twentieth and today's the twentieth."

It was improbable that anyone was within hearing distance of Trotter's murmured words, but still the lieutenant played the role as carefully as North; it was the way the pair did things.

"T'hell with 'em, then," North boomed. "Do they think I got nothin' more important to do than—"

"I believe someone's coming now, sir," Trotter broke in.

Hugh turned to see a man burst out of the door of the waiting room for private planes and rush across the apron toward Kenny and him. The newcomer wore a blue blazer with a club insignia at the breast pocket, light slacks, and white shoes. On his head was a yachting cap. Closer to, he revealed himself as Wesley Grafton, round-faced, heavy-eyed, a man in his early fifties whose face bore no distinguishing features beyond a somewhat brushy mustache and the tired eyes.

He thrust out a hand toward North when he was still ten feet away. "Mr. Gregory, I'm terribly sorry I'm late. I'm Wesley Grafton."

North met the millionaire's hand and bore down on a crushing grip. "Well, hi!" he cried. "Just tellin' Kenny-boy here—

he's my secretary—just tellin' him I was afraid you forgot us or some'n."

Grafton made an effort to smile as he mopped at his forehead with a handkerchief. "No, no, of course not. Frightfully sorry. My fault. Coming over from the island my boat acted up—the damned low-grade gas the natives unload on us— and we were late getting into the dock. Then we had to pick up a friend of Barbara's—Mrs. Grafton's—who came down on an airliner and—well, with one thing and another we ran 'way behind schedule.' My apologies."

"Why, hell, that's all right," Hugh thundered. "Nothin' that can't be cured by a drink. Say, Grafton, what's this deal you want to talk to me about? What's all the mystery business?"

The millionaire cast a startled look about him, found nobody who appeared to be eavesdropping, and replied in a hushed voice. "We can discuss that when we get to the island, Mr. Gregory," he said.

"Sure," North hollered. "Anything you say. But call me Yahoo, for God's sake. This Mister Gregory business makes me nervous. Only time anybody calls me Mister Gregory is when they want to take me to the cleaners." He whooped an ear-splitting laugh. "I hope you fellers don't plan on doin' that to me," he cried.

Grafton looked appalled but he managed another weak smile. "I think we know better than to try that, Mr.—er— Yahoo," he said.

North told himself this Wesley Grafton was an odd type to be such a figure in the financial world. North had been well filled in on Grafton's personal appearance as well as his entire background, from nursery school up, but still he had not expected quite the man he met now. Grafton had played college football and yet now he appeared dumpy, soft. The uncertain light did not give Hugh opportunity for too close study of Grafton's features but enough to see that the millionaire wore eye bags that would have gone better with a man much older. Even in this light, Hugh could see that Grafton was deeply tanned, but the sun's coloring had not imparted any especially healthy glow.

An ill-lighted airport apron was not the best place for the G-2 colonel to probe a man's expression, but Hugh found in what he saw and in the timbre of Grafton's voice a note that might reflect many things: compulsive drive, cupidity, unrelenting ambition—or fear.

"So glad you could come down," Grafton was saying. "I hope we won't have to keep you long. The deal is all set up, actually—just a question of your going over the facts and figures and making your decision." He gave a barked laugh, surprising after his earlier painful smiles. "We certainly hope you decide to throw in with Townley and me."

"Who's Townley?" North demanded bluntly.

"Townley Ward," Grafton explained. "Ever met him?"

"Not unless he dug dirt in the state of Utah all his life, podner," North boomed. "With a name like that, I don't reckon he did. Sounds like another society feller to me."

"Oh, you'll like him," Grafton said. "Great fellow. He's got one of the best brains—but here I am talking along like an old woman and I imagine you'd like to get through customs and on your way, eh?"

"What I'd like is a drink," Hugh boomed. "They got a bar in this airport?"

"Why, yes, but—ah—why not wait until we get aboard my boat? I don't know what kind of liquor they serve here but I've got some rather special stock on *Amphitrite.*"

"On which?"

"*Amphitrite.* That's my boat. It's over at the St. George's Yacht Club, a stone's throw from here."

North wagged his head admiringly. "Fancy name," he said. "*Amphitrite.*" He turned and shot the question at Kenny, grinning inwardly. "What's it mean, Kenny-boy? You oughta know, you bein' a college boy."

Trotter fooled him. "Amphitrite was the wife of Neptune, sir," he shot back. "Daughter of Nereus and Doris."

Hugh turned to Grafton. "How about that, podner?" he cried. "Ain't he somethin', though? Earns his pay every time he opens his mouth, prett' near. C'mon, let's get goin'. I'm thirsty."

Grafton headed North toward the customs office, Kenny trailing. By that time, the steward of Wildcat Bill Allenby's plane had wheeled in the bogus Gregory's baggage (on loan from the real Yahoo; alligator with solid gold mountings) and the transit through customs required only a few minutes, even though the customs officers were bewildered and enchanted by North's loud declarations concerning the value of the things they inspected.

"Careful with them things, podner," the make-believe uranium king would cry. "That's a three-hundred-dollar pair of boots you got there—don't bend 'em."

Out of the corner of his eye the G-2 colonel noticed that Wesley Grafton mopped his brow frequently during the brief stay in the customs shed, even though the night was not that warm. North wondered if Grafton was regretting his decision to include Yahoo Gregory's millions in this deal that was on the fire and came to the conclusion that a man like Grafton could stand a lot of public embarrassment to lay hands on the money he wanted to swing a history-making deal.

The customs inspection finally finished, Grafton seized North's gaudy elbow. "I've got a car outside to take us to St. George's," he said.

"Got to see about my airplane first," North protested. "Can't leave her just settin' out there—"

"All taken care of, Mr. Gregory," Trotter put in. "The crew has orders to stand by until you need them."

The colonel beamed down at Grafton again. "Y'see?" he asked. "That's my Kenny-boy—looks after everything. I can't get used to havin' things done for me instead of takin' care of everything myself like I had to do for forty years, prett' near."

"Er—yes," Grafton murmured. "This way."

The car (and Hugh North remembered a day before World War II when an automobile had been anathema on these islands) turned out to be a sleek Lincoln chauffeured by a dark-skinned Bermudian who silently, skillfully, tooled the car through the quiet streets of Hamilton and over the bridge that connected Grand Bermuda with St. George's Island. Here there was even less activity than in Hamilton, and as the sedan rolled through the Olde Towne's main square the streets were virtually deserted. The mooring slips at the St. George's Yacht Club were silent and dark except for one long, graceful, flying-bridge cruiser where lights showed and a figure in white waited at the gangplank.

"There's my boat," Wesley Grafton said in the offhand manner of a person accustomed to such costly luxuries. "It's a short trip to my island. I hope you'll be comfortable there—Bermuda's not as fashionable as Cat Cay and some other places these days, but my family's been coming here for years and my daughter, Gail, loves Plunder Island and Freebooter's Hall so much that we haven't moved on with the rest."

"Plunder Island, hey?" North bellowed. "You call it that 'cause you plundered the dough to buy it?"

Grafton permitted himself a tight smile. "Some people have accused me of it, as a matter of fact," he acknowledged; "but it so happens that this place was named long before we Graftons came here. It dates back to the old days."

"And Freebooter's Hall, too?" North pursued.

"No," Grafton said. "I named that myself when I had the new place built."

"Means pirates, don't it? Yah-haw-haw, that's a good one! I better watch myself with a feller that admits he's a pirate by the name of his house. And what about that deal, anyway? Can you tell me now what's cookin'?"

Grafton nodded his head toward the silent chauffeur as the car rolled out on the broad pier toward the waiting *Amphitrite*. "Later, when we're alone," he said.

Hugh snorted but made no further protest. The Lincoln came to a halt by the gangplank and Grafton got out, turning to lend a hand to North who scorned the proffered aid. The G-2 colonel thumped his boots across the pier toward the man in white with the yachtsman's cap and stuck out a broad hand. "Hi," he said without preliminaries. "I'm Yahoo Gregory. Looks like you're skipper of thisyere boat so where do they keep the likker?"

The dark-skinned skipper accepted Hugh's handshake after a moment's hesitation, then raised his fingers to his cap visor.

"Welcome aboard, sar," he said in a mellifluous voice. "I'll see to de luggage, sar."

"Fine, fine," North said, "but answer my question first. Where's the bar?"

"I'll show you," Grafton offered, his voice nettled. "Let's go aboard and meet Miss Pendleton. She's the young lady I mentioned, Mrs. Grafton's house guest."

He crossed to the boat beside North and guided the pseudo-prospector-made-millionaire through the long cockpit into a spacious cabin. "Sue Anne," he said to the blonde who sat in a deep wicker chair opposite the cabin door, "this is Mr. Gregory, Miss Pendleton. Of Macon, Georgia."

"Call me Yahoo," North grinned and added, to express aloud what he knew Kenny Trotter was saying silently, "Miss, you're the prettiest thing I've seen since they took the horse cars off Main Street."

[4]

Miss Sue Anne Pendleton was a blonde. Decidedly. The lamps of the luxuriously fitted cabin made her hair a sleek cap of spun gold and her complexion was all that a Georgia blonde's should be—ripe peaches and thick cream. Her eyes were blue and enormous, and as she looked up at North the G-2 colonel found himself wondering two things: whether this girl could be quite as empty-headed as her baby-doll stare indicated and whether she had deliberately crossed her legs that high or did not know how much she had on view.

Miss Pendleton blinked (Hugh told himself he would have to get used to people blinking at first sight of Yahoo Gregory) and extended a slender, red-tipped hand. "I'm soooo glad to meet you," she purred in a Southern drawl impossible to transcribe. "I've heard soooo much about you, Mr. Gregory."

"Yahoo," North corrected, "and don't believe a damn word of what you heard about me. Pack of lies, most of it."

"Oh, but it was all goooood," Miss Pendleton cooed. "Honestly, you're the most fabulous man I ever heard of. That time you went to Las Vegas and bought the gambling casino 'cause you didn't like the limits they put on the games."

"Hell, that was nothin', Miss," Hugh bellowed. "Ever tell you about the time I told somebody I flew my own plane? Feller asks what's so great about that, lotta people fly their own plane. In their livin' room, I asked him? Yaw-haw-haw! How's about that drink, Grafton?"

He left Sue Anne giggling dutifully and turned toward Grafton as the millionaire headed for a bar set in a corner of the cabin. "What would you like?" Grafton asked.

"Bourbon 'n' branchwater," North cried. "Light dustin' of water—just enough to keep it respectable, hey, podner?"

Behind him, he heard Kenny Trotter introducing himself to the gorgeous Miss Pendleton. North did not know whether private secretaries were supposed to introduce themselves to their boss's new acquaintances or not, but he let it pass; he knew he could no more keep Kenny from approaching a girl that pretty than he could make water flow uphill.

The colonel took the drink Grafton mixed and flourished it. "Look out below," he announced, and tossed it off. He repressed a shudder; Wesley Grafton might have the best bourbon obtainable, but Scotch was Hugh's drink and Scotch was something that the real Yahoo Gregory sneered at as a sissy's potion. The G-2 man told himself that not the easiest part of this job was going to be the swallowing of enormous quantities of bourbon, in keeping with Yahoo's character, and at the same time managing somehow to stay sober enough to carry out his official duties. The days of potted palms in drawing rooms being past, North said silently that he would have to find something else to pour his bourbon into, somehow, when the going got rough.

He took a second bourbon-and from Grafton and noted that the millionaire had finished his own Scotch and soda at a speed that matched the spurious Yahoo's. *Does he always toss 'em down this fast, or is he under a strain?* North headed for a chair beside Sue Anne, managing to shoulder Kenny Trotter aside as he did.

"Go fix yourself a drink, son," he told his aide. "But not too stiff—somebody's got to be on their feet in case I suddenly get took drunk." And he laughed at his own hilarious announcement.

Once seated, he waved his glass at Grafton. "How about now?" he asked. "Can we talk business now, seein' we can keep it all in the family, y'might say?"

Grafton frowned and shook his head. There was a second's silence and then Sue Anne cried: "Oh, go right ahead, if you want to. Don't worry about me. It'll all be over my head. I'm afraid I'm pretty stupid, when you come right down to it."

"Personally, I hate smart women," North said. "Gimme a cute little thing like you that don't worry her pretty head about menfolks' business every time."

The boat captain appeared at the cockpit hatch, saluting. "Bags all aboard, sar," he told Grafton. "Cast off?"

Grafton nodded and the skipper left. From outside came the sounds of the yacht club's attendants handling *Amphitrite's* bow and stern lines.

"What's your skipper's name?" North asked. "Seems like a right able feller."

Grafton seemed to seize on the subject gratefully. "Oh, he's able enough," he said. "His name's John Cavendish but everybody calls him Creepy. Notice his features? Not Negroid at all. Creepy's descended from the Pequots of St. David's Island."

"Pequots?" Hugh asked. "Indians, ain't they?"

"Yes," Grafton nodded. "Back around 1675, a lot of Pequot warriors were captured in Connecticut during King Philip's War and were shipped out here to Bermuda as slaves. The colonists here tried everything but the Indians simply wouldn't do slaves' work. Like most New England Indians, they were very fierce, very proud. It wound up that they'd—ah—cooperate in only two lines of work, whaling and boat-building. They're excellent watermen to this day."

As Grafton spoke, the big cruiser's engines thrummed and the boat began moving out of her slip into the dark and motionless harbor of St. George's Island. *Amphitrite* was a smooth-running, ably handled craft, and Hugh marveled at the way this Creepy maneuvered the cruiser among the tightly packed moored vessels in the harbor, never overwheeling, cutting buoys with less than an inch to spare, but never brushing *Amphitrite's* white sides with vessel, buoy, or spar that he passed.

Through the hatch, the skipper was visible at the wheel, totally expressionless, dark-skinned, hawk-eyed, high-cheek-boned. The bill of his yachting cap shaded his eyes from the binnacle light, but Hugh had seen them when he had met the Pequot-Bermudian on the quay and he knew they were bright, black, and proud. And how did this descendant of New England Pequot chiefs like the nickname "Creepy"? How did he like his employer speaking in front of him as though he were some strange specimen instead of a human being?

Hugh North was no sociologist nor yet an amateur psychologist, but he had the idea that John Cavendish, "Creepy," held no love for his boss.

Without seeming to, he scrutinized Grafton and Miss Pendleton. Sue Anne needed to be reminded that she was a big girl now, but with the pair of legs that she owned it would be a shame to have her cover them. Grafton's pouched eyes made a valiant effort to stay away from gleaming knee and beyond but failed, always returning to the charms so carelessly exposed.

"I 'clare, I'm so thrilled about seein' Barby again!" the blonde was saying. She turned to Hugh. "Barby's Barbara Winslow and—oops!" She clapped a hand to her full red lips and stared in horror at her host, Grafton.

The millionaire made hard work of it but he managed a smile. "Quite all right," he said in a strained voice. "Natural mistake."

"But I'm a complete *idiot!*" Sue Anne wailed. "And all the way down here I've been remindin' myself that Barby's Mrs. *Grafton* now, not Barby Winslow."

She appealed to North in pretty distress. "Aren't I the *dumbest* thing?" she mourned.

"Think nothin' of it," Hugh said expansively. "Keepin' track of ladies' married names is a job, these days."

"Oh, but I should have known better," Miss Pendleton cried. "You see, Barby was married to Ted Winslow before—before the divorce. And here I am, forgettin' it right away. Oh dear, you won't like me at all, Mr. Grafton."

The millionaire's face was dull red under his tan and his smile went no further than his teeth, under the bristling mustache. "Don't let it bother you," he muttered. To North he explained: "Sue Anne was my wife's closest friend at college."

So Barbara must be about half your age, then.

" 'Deed I was," Sue Anne nodded. "Barby was Barbara James then, the most beautiful girl at Smith, everybody said. And tell me, Mr. Grafton, how's Barby's cute lil ole brother, Terry?"

"Fine," Grafton said sourly.

"And—and your daughter—Gail, isn't it?"

North saw the millionaire relax for the first time since he had met the man. Grafton's smile was genuine as he replied to the question. "Gail's just fine," he said. "Grows prettier every day, or at least I think so."

"Oh, I've seen her pictures and she *is* beautiful," Sue Anne said enthusiastically. "Is what I read in somebody's column true? I mean, is she goin' to marry that—that fish expert?"

Fish expert! Even Hugh North started at that one. His dossier on Grafton had included the fact that he had recently married the wealthy and beautiful Barbara James Winslow after Barbara's surprise Reno divorce, and he knew Grafton had a twenty-five-year-old daughter, Gail, by his first wife, dead for three years. However, there had been nothing about any fish expert paying court to Gail Grafton.

The millionaire's face was an ugly mottled picture of angered embarrassment as he jerked out: "No, it's not true! Gail will never marry that Gibbons fellow if I can help it!"

With which he sought North in what seemed close to desperation, passing his handkerchief over his forehead again. "How about another drink?"

"Why, sure," North said promptly while his stomach quivered. To Sue Anne he explained: "I can't walk on two legs—I got centipede blood in my veins." And he threw back his head and gave that hideous laugh again.

Sue Anne Pendleton, however, was not to be disposed of that easily. Still wearing her I-don't-know-what-it's-all-about expression, she said: "Mama almost didn't let me come to visit you, Mr. Grafton. After that girl drowned—your secretary, wasn't she?—Mama was afraid it wasn't safe at Freebooter's Hall. It *is* quite safe, isn't it? I mean the swimming, of course."

[5]

Hugh was interested in the reaction the Georgia blonde's question brought from Wesley Grafton. The G-2 colonel saw Grafton's face turn purple, then fade to a washed-out gray-brown as the millionaire stared at the leggy blonde. "Safe? Why, of course it's safe," he finally managed to growl.

Sue Anne waved graceful hands. "That's what I told Mama," she chirruped, "but she's such a sweet ole worry-wart. She said your secretary was supposed to be a marvelous swimmer and yet *she* got drowned and what would happen to me, a little ole dog-paddler that can hardly stay afloat?"

Hugh thought it time to put Yahoo Gregory into this situation. "What's this about your secretary, Grafton?" he boomed. "You have some trouble down here?"

The putty-faced millionaire made brushing motions with his meaty hands. "No—well, yes. My secretary, Miss Forthier, went swimming at night last week and—she must have been caught in the tide at the Pass or something. Anyway, she disappeared, drowned."

"Well, say now," the colonel said heavily, "that's tough. Mighty upsettin'. You reckon we oughta have this conference at your place with everybody so shook up over this thing?"

"Oh, it's quite all right," Grafton said hurriedly as his color returned. "It was a shock, certainly, but—well, it wasn't as though Judy—Miss Forthier—was a member of the family. Tragedy and all that, but the world must go on, eh?"

"Uh-huh," Hugh nodded. "How'd it happen, anyway? And you were goin' to make me a drink, remember?"

Grafton took North's glass and repaired to the bar, bracing himself against the slight swell that was beginning to move *Amphitrite*. The millionaire spoke over his shoulder.

"She went swimming at night," he explained. "She—well, I'm afraid she had too many drinks. There was quite a party going on, folks over from the other islands and an orchestra—celebrating my daughter's birthday, as a matter of fact. Nobody missed Judy until after the party was over and then—then somebody remembered hearing her say she wanted a swim to clear her head. Damn fool thing to do under any circumstances but to go up to the Pass—well, it was a terrible mistake."

"You find the body?" North asked bluntly.

"Well, no. No, they didn't. Not to be expected, really. You see there's a regular millrace through the Pass between Plunder Island and the next adjoining island, Castle Island. Used to be all one long ago, before a hurricane made a gut, and the tide moves through there fast, in or out. Judy knew better than to swim anywhere near there. Must have been tight as a tick, poor kid." Grafton suddenly drained his glass and turned to the bar again.

"If you didn't find the body, how d'you know she drowned?" Hugh asked. "Just 'cause she said she was goin' swimmin' don't mean she went."

"They found her clothes on the shore near the Pass," Grafton explained in a voice barely audible over the noise made by the ice dropping into his glass. "She—I guess that's why Judy went so far south of the regular beach to swim. She didn't want to be caught swimming nude, I guess."

He turned back from the bar. "It was purely a tragic accident," he said firmly before he raised his glass to drink.

. "Castle Island off de bow, Plunder to starb'd," Creepy called down in his liquid voice.

2.

THERE WAS no moon but the night was clear, the stars bright, as *Amphitrite* crept in toward the two islands ahead. Starlight cast a soft glow over sea and land and permitted Hugh an entrancing view of the two stretches of land—Castle Island to the south of a narrow cut, Plunder Island, by far the larger, lying to the north.

A crumbling ruin dominated Castle Island. It stood on the southernmost point of the rockpile thrusting up out of the sea, a ghostly heap of masonry that still suggested the power and splendor it once had possessed. A tower heaved its bulk up into the night and about the thick spire were the remains of battlements that once must have defended these waters against pirates and Spanish galleons.

"De ole fort, sar," Creepy was saying softly. "Folks call it King's Castle now, sar. In de olden times they say she mounted over forty guns and a whole regiment of troops were quartered there. When it's light I take out to the ocean side where there's de better view."

Sue Anne Pendleton clasped Hugh's arm, ostensibly to steady herself against the boat's motion but accidentally or otherwise employing the move to impress against the colonel the softness of her rounded excellence. "Isn't it *romantic?*" she cried. "Just think what that ole fort must have seen in all the years it's been sitting there."

"Sure need a hell of a lot of dough to fix up now, though," North, as Yahoo Gregory, commented. "Don't look hardly livable, does it?"

"Nobody live dere now but de rats and de ghosts," Creepy said.

"Never mind the ghosts," Wesley Grafton barked. "And don't get caught in that rough water off the Pass, dammit! Head straight for the pier."

"Yes, sar," Creepy said tonelessly and bucked over the wheel so sharply that *Amphitrite* caught a wave broadside, another, and staggered for a moment before recovering.

"Watch what the hell you're doing!" Grafton crackled.

"Yes, sar, but you said de straight course for de pier, sar. We was quarterin' in but when you said straight course for de pier I had to—"

"Never mind," Grafton cut in, scowling. Hardly bothering to lower his voice, the multimillionaire said to North: "Damned natives—they do anything to make us uncomfortable without quite stepping over the line far enough to be fired."

Creepy could not have helped hearing what Grafton said and again Hugh North wondered why the Pequot-Bermudian stood for an employer like Grafton. Were expert boatmen such as Creepy so common in the Bermudas? Or did Grafton soothe the hurts of his contemptuous tongue with the wages he paid?

Amphitrite slid into a small lagoon and up to a coral block pier opposite the lights ashore that marked Freebooter's Hall. The cruiser gently touched a padded piling and immediately two men, both clad in white ducks and singlets, leapt aboard, one at the bow, the other astern, and made her fast, silently and adroitly. Creepy cut the engines and stood at the landing mat to give a hand to Sue Anne Pendleton's elbow as she went up onto the dock.

North and Grafton followed the girl up onto the pier with the silent Kenny Trotter trailing. Grafton gestured toward the pavilion that raised its roof halfway down the pier toward shore.

"I imagine they'll be having drinks down here—yes, there's Townley. And Mrs. Grafton."

The couple, millionaire playboy and hostess of Plunder Island, had arisen from the deck chairs they had been occupying and now stood awaiting the others' approach. Shaded lights set about the pavilion gave Hugh enough illumination to study the features of Mrs. Grafton and Townley Ward as he was introduced. They made a striking pair.

Barbara James Winslow Grafton was a tall, Junoesque brunette, patrician of face and figure and yet softened by marks of the sensualist, the full lips, the curving haunch, and deep breast. Hugh had seen photographs of this woman, many of them, but none had presented her striking beauty in its living vibrancy.

North thought: *No wonder Grafton went mad over her—so mad he couldn't rest until he'd won her away from Winslow.*

That posed a question, too: why had Barbara James sloughed off a handsome husband her own age to marry Wesley Grafton? Money? But Barbara came from a staggeringly wealthy family in her own right and Winslow had had plenty of money—nothing like Grafton but enough to give Barbara anything she wanted. Yet, if rumors were true, Winslow had accepted a huge sum from Grafton to let his wife get the Reno divorce with a minimum of scandal—did these too-rich people always reach for more money, no matter what?

The G-2 colonel watched Mrs. Grafton as the brunette greeted her Smith College classmate with an enthusiasm that bordered on the hysterical. The two young women, one the striking brunette, the other the dazzling blonde, embraced each other with squeals and babbled happy incoherencies for a moment before Barbara Grafton turned toward Hugh.

She blinked as they all did when they saw North's array, but she made a supreme effort to be cordial to this red-faced nobody from nowhere whose pockets held money her husband wanted to use. "Nice to have you, Mr. Gregory," she said. "I hope you have a pleasant stay on Plunder Island."

"Been fine, so far," North said cheerfully. "Seein' another gal who's pretty like Sue Anne don't hurt none."

"Why—thank you," Barbara said uncertainly.

"And this is Townley Ward," Wesley Grafton continued.

Ward had none of Barbara Grafton's polite reserve or if he had, he shucked it now. The young man fairly thrust himself past his hostess to extend his hand. "So nice to meet you, Mr. Gregory," he said. "Been wanting to meet you for a long time. Heard a lot about you, of course."

North grinned. "Guess everybody's heard about me," he admitted, shamelessly. "And call me Yahoo. I come quicker that way."

He accepted Ward's hand and felt his fingers caught in a bone-crushing grip. Townley Ward was very fit and he wanted everyone to know it; his handshake was more a test of strength than a friendly amenity.

If there was anything Hugh North despised it was the knuckle-cracker, the hand-wringer, and the G-2 colonel welcomed the role that let him react in kind. He had his share of steel in his hand and he brought it into full play now; the two men stood locked in a beartrap grip for a moment, and it was Townley Ward who silently cried "uncle" as he ended the contest. As his hand dropped away, North was conscious of Ward's respectful glance; it would be a long time before that young man would try to grind North's knuckles again.

"Hey, Wes," North bawled, to cover the brief silence, "how about makin' me one?"

Grafton, on his way to the portable bar set up at one side of the pavilion, hesitated and then nodded.

"You weren't tryin' to sneak one in on me, were you?" Hugh guffawed. "Never try that when Yahoo Gregory's around—he can hear a bottle bein' picked up forty miles away."

The G-2 man sensed, rather than saw, Barbara Grafton's grimace of distaste. Poor Barbara, she was going to be hard put to it to maintain her correctness if Yahoo stayed long at Freebooter's Hall. North loathed the things his role called on him to do but a study of the real Yahoo's history had convinced him that to be any softer of voice, any less ill-mannered, would be to make him suspect in the eyes of anyone who had made even a casual investigation of Yahoo's background. And these sharpshooting multimillionaires certainly must have gotten the complete picture of Gregory before they had approached the uranium man. So on with the show.

He plumped himself down in a chair beside Barbara Grafton and glanced shoreward. "Nice little place you got here," he said generously. "Nice boat, too. Yep, you look like you're doin' all right." He called across the pavilion to Kenny Trotter who was edging closer to Sue Anne Pendleton. "Kenny-boy, suppose you run up to our room and make yourself busy with them reports they want back in Salt Lake. Supposed to have 'em in Washington by Monday and here it is Wednesday, already. Wes, can you get somebody to show my secretary where we're supposed to bunk?"

"Sure," Grafton said and swigged his drink down. "Matter of fact, I've got to go up to the house myself; I'll show Trotter your rooms. You just sit here and get acquainted, Yahoo. Townley, will you take care of the drinks?"

"And if you see Gail, Wesley," Barbara Grafton called after her husband, "remind her that we have guests." The voice was as smooth and polished as a dagger.

Grafton went up the pier with Kenny Trotter. A moment later one of the servants trundled a hand truck past, carrying Sue Anne's and North's luggage up to the house. Townley Ward busied himself at the bar, fixing Hugh and the girl from Macon their drinks, getting a refill for Barbara and himself.

"Long time no see, Townley," Sue Anne said as the young millionaire handed her her drink. "How've you been?"

"Busy," Ward said briefly. He turned with almost deliberate insult and faced North again. "Have an easy flight over from New York?" he asked.

Why should he be so cold to Sue Anne if he hasn't seen her in such a long time? That was almost a slap in the face. Is Sue Anne coming here at an inconvenient time for Ward's plans?

Sue Anne, however, seemed oblivious to the slight. She cradled her drink, her smile never faltering.

"Okay, I guess," the colonel said in reply to the younger man's question. "I got the habit of fallin' asleep in a plane so I couldn't tell you for sure whether it was rough or smooth." Of such things was the dossier on Yahoo Gregory composed; Yahoo always fell asleep in planes.

"I imagine it would have to be pretty rough to upset you, Mr. Gregory," Barbara Grafton said sweetly.

"Well, hell, I had it rough all my life," Hugh laughed. "I bounced my tail off a mule's backbone too long to worry about a little bumpy air." He pulled mightily at his drink. "You ever rode a mule, Barby?" he asked.

The "Barby" at such short notice jolted Mrs. Grafton but she smiled gamely. "No," she said. "It must be a fascinating sport."

"Well, you take a mule, now," Hugh said and was off on a windy dissertation about the mule, its virtues and shortcomings. And while he talked (this was a trick it had taken North years to master) he studied Townley Ward critically, letting his tongue ramble on while he went over Ward with all his keen faculties of observation and deduction.

The young rich man had draped his elegant self in a deck chair opposite, his tall drink in one powerful hand. He was a strikingly handsome figure and knew it. His wedge-shouldered frame was encased in a light-blue silk dinner jacket, cummerbund, and evening trousers, and the light from a bracket lamp over him illumined a face that had all the attributes of rugged male comeliness, the firm jaw, the chiseled nose, dark curly hair, wide-spaced eyes, perfect teeth.

Hugh knew more than to let his near-prettiness mislead him. Already credited with some master strokes of finance that had surprised (and sometimes ruined) his elders in the marts of money, Townley Ward looked like nothing more than the perpetual undergraduate, the collegian reluctant to grow up and leave the campus and fraternity house, football stadium and prom. Actually, he was possessed of a steel-trap mind, an intelligence that went oddly with that Adonic face.

"Never give Ward an advantage in bridge, business, or badminton or he'll murder you," Hugh's General had told him. "And don't play it too easy with Wesley Grafton, either. Neither of them got where they are by being dopes. Make one slip and chances are that one or the other will spot you for a phoney, so watch yourself."

Which, Colonel North reminded himself—all this in the midst of the oration concerning the habits, quirks, and contradictions of the *species mulus*—was good advice, especially worthy of remembering in this situation. The chief danger in playing Yahoo Gregory, he knew, was in bearing down too heavily with the histrionics. The real Yahoo might be a weatherbeaten extrovert of renowned intemperate tongue but he also was a shrewd old boy who was no fool, although he delighted in acting like one. Ward and Grafton should know pretty well where the real Gregory would stop playing the clown, and it was up to North to fix that line and avoid going over it. At the same time, Ward and Grafton must expect Yahoo to act like Yahoo most of the time, mouthy, objectionable, and would be quick to detect any holes in North's pose. This mission was something of a tightrope job—with the tightrope walker drinking gallons of bourbon 'n' branchwater as he teetered.

The colonel finished his lecture on mules, and Sue Anne grabbed the chance to get in a word. "Barby, I've got fifty million things to talk over with you. Everybody you know told me to say hello to you and tell you this and that. What I mean is, can't we get off someplace and let down our hair? I'm sure Mr. Yahoo and Townley will excuse us."

North expected Barbara to leap for the escape hatch but she did not. "Oh, we'll have days and days to talk, darling," she said gently. "Townley and Wes and Mr. Gregory will be knee-deep in business from tomorrow breakfast on, and they won't want to be bothered once they start, so we'd better take advantage of their charming company now. We'll be positively snarled at once they go into conference. I know from experience."

"Catch me snarlin' at a beautiful woman like you," North scoffed. "You just yell for Yahoo, Barby, and I'll come a-runnin', no matter what kind of business we're messin' with." He looked about him, sniffed the perfumed night air. "Besides," he added, "I didn't come all the way down here just to talk business. No, sir. I figgered on havin' a little fun while I'm here, too. First time I ever been outta the country, and I don't want to go back and tell the folks I didn't do nothin' but look over figgers and read prospectuses."

"Well, hooray," Sue Anne crowed. "So you see, Barby, it's not going to be like you thought at all."

"There'll be plenty of time for fun," Townley Ward put in. "Matter of fact, Creepy's got it all arranged for us to see a Gombey dance tomorrow night."

"Gombey dance?" North asked.

"A native celebration," Ward explained. "Related to the Haitian voodoo rites, I believe, only these have been tamed down somewhat."

"Tamed down?" North asked. "You mean with all the kick out of it?"

"Wellll," Ward drawled, "I understand that sometimes they put on a little livelier version. Creepy might arrange it—I understand he's a big wheel with the natives. But it might shock you, Yahoo."

The G-2 colonel gave vent to the guffaw that doubtless had earned Gregory his nickname. "Shock me? Podner, you oughta seen some of the shows I seen in Mexico. They had one—uh—no, I guess not." He grinned at Barbara Grafton. "I don't guess I know you ladies well enough, yet," he explained.

"Oh, go ahead and tell us, Yahoo," Sue Anne urged. "We're not babies, for heaven's sake."

"No," Barbara Grafton said firmly. To Hugh she said: "Don't expect too much of a peep show at a Gombey dance, Mr. Gregory. They're rather unusual the first time one sees them but they can get dull, too—like everything else around here."

"Oh, come now, Barbara," Ward protested. "Plunder Island's not as bad as that."

"It's dull," the brunette repeated. "Dull, dull, dull. Nothing but one damned business conference after another. Here I sit in one of the most romantic settings on the face of the globe and listen to talk about debentures and loans and cartels and monopolies and God knows what, until I think I'll go mad."

She turned in her chair and leaned toward the colonel, so close that Hugh caught the smell of alcohol on her breath. "Believe me, Yahoo, your talk about mules was refreshing.

You're refreshing. You're the first male human being who's come to Freebooter's Hall in a long time. Welcome."

Oh-oh, Hugh told himself; *it's been a long evening and milady has had one too many.* Aloud, he stumbled: "Well, now, ma'am, I aim to talk about somethin' else besides business—even mules. You and me oughta get along real good."

"I'm sure we will," Barbara Grafton said, back to her polished steel manner. "Townley, fix me another drink like a dear."

Ward attempted an easy laugh as he got out of his deck chair. It came out uneasy. "You'll have Yahoo thinking we're a crowd of lushes, Barbara," he chided. To North, he added: "The lady's in one of her moods, that's all."

"I keep thinking of that girl," Barbara Grafton said quietly, almost absently. "What really happened to Judy Forthier?"

[2]

There was a certain sadness in Barbara Grafton's voice, and a thread of fear, too, that quickened Hugh North's hopes. Perhaps a break was at hand, within minutes of reaching Plunder Island, where Counterintelligence Agent Judy Forthier had been snatched from sight, where men of money hatched a scheme that might endanger America's security.

The character of Yahoo Gregory let him rush in where a more prudent man might have hesitated. "Yeah," he said, "what happened to that girl, anyway? Sue Anne, here, said her mama was worried about it bein' safe for her here."

Barbara's dark-eyed face swung toward the blonde from Georgia. "Safe? Of course it's safe!" she said sharply. "Where in the world did your mother get the ridiculous idea that it might not be, Sue Anne?"

The blonde squirmed in her wicker chair as the eyes of the others pinned themselves on her. "Oh, you know Mama," she said lamely. "She wouldn't be happy unless she was worryin' about something silly."

"And this is silly," Barbara said, her voice rising. "Because poor Judy was reckless and got caught in the current in the Pass doesn't mean there's any danger for any of us. I never heard of such a thing."

There was an embarrassed pause and then North said: "You'd think they'd have found her body by now. Don't drowned people come to the surface after three days or somethin' like that?"

"Not necessarily," Townley Ward said soberly, "and, besides, you haven't seen the current in the Pass where Judy went swimming. Her body must have been carried miles out to sea before she was even missed. That's what the police think."

"You mean the cops have already closed the case?" the colonel asked.

"Of course," Ward said swiftly, before Barbara could speak. "Inspector Boyd—he's the top police authority around here—assured us we wouldn't be bothered any more except"—he hesitated, wishing he had not come this far, but had to go on —"unless there's the question of identifying a corpse."

North pulled at his drink, finished it, and rattled the ice in his glass as he looked down at it, his face shadowed by the brim of the sombrero he had not doffed in all this time. "Seems like pretty sloppy police work to me," he said bluntly. "Gal disappears from a wild party—"

"But it wasn't a wild party," Barbara Grafton cried indignantly. "Just a few people in from St. George's and one or two couples over from the nearby islands. People like us. It was no brawl, for heaven's sake."

"Well, I didn't mean it was," North hedged. "But you was drinkin', Wes said, and this gal must've been pretty tight if she thought she had to go swimmin' to sober up and then went somewheres she hadn't oughta gone swimmin' at all. And nobody missed her for a long time—that don't sound like no church social to me. If I was the police, I'd—"

Barbara Grafton broke in, her voice cold, incisive. "But you're not, Mr. Gregory," she said. "And please don't try to play detective or anything like that. I—I know how important you are to my husband's plans and I don't want to offend you, but I must tell you that I don't want you or anyone else trying to make some sort of a—a—big case out of this accident. The police have called it an accident, Mr. Gregory. Don't let your —ah—impulsiveness try to make anything else out of it, please."

"Well, now," Hugh said in tones of outraged dignity, "I was only sayin'—"

"Hold it, Yahoo," Townley Ward said swiftly. "Here comes her sister."

North glanced up the pier. Coming toward the pavilion was a girl in a filmy dress, a tall, slender young woman who walked with bowed head. Hugh eyed her carefully. This, then, was the girl Counterintelligence was doubtful about; this was the sister who had suddenly appeared out of nowhere.

"It's Judy's sister, Patricia Forthier," Barbara explained in a smothered aside. "She flew down right after the accident, poor girl. I don't know what she thinks we could have done but— oh, I suppose it's my imagination but she seems to be blaming us for her sister's death."

"Quiet," Townley hissed.

Hugh North kept his hat on, kept his seat, the empty drink in his hand, but as Patricia Forthier entered the pavilion he eyed her thoroughly, wondering.

Was this woman really Judy Forthier's sister or was she, like Colonel Hugh North himself, playing a role in the drama being enacted on Plunder Island?

[3]

The woman who called herself Patricia Forthier turned out to be a strong-faced person with a firm chin, sharp nose, and brown hair in a neat coiffure. Hugh North had seen photographs of Rogers' agent, Judy Forthier, and knew she had been a delicious copper blonde of the cuddly type; if Patricia really was Judy's sister there certainly was no resemblance.

The colonel lumbered to his feet as the newcomer approached the group, his gaze bland but missing nothing. Patricia's eyes were red and swollen as she came into the light, but that did little to convince North that she was the McCoy; too often had he seen irritants used by actresses to induce copious weeping.

"Come sit over here, dear," Barbara Grafton said in a voice far different from the tone she had been using—a quiet, sympathetic invitation. "Townley, fix Miss Forthier a drink. What will you have, Patricia?"

"Nothing, thanks," the young woman said. Her voice was low-timbred, subdued. "I—I wouldn't have bothered you except Mr. Grafton met me in the house and insisted I join you."

"Of course," Townley Ward cried. "And you must have a drink; it will do you good. Let me fix you a Scotch."

While the young man in the blue dinner jacket busied himself at the bar, Barbara introduced Patricia to Sue Anne and North. The bereaved girl acknowledged the introductions with a nod and a muttered word.

"I'm so sorry about your sister," Sue Anne said. "But maybe —well, maybe she was picked up by a boat or somethin'; you never can tell."

"Sure," Hugh said, back in character. "Heard about a feller one time got carried out into the Gulf of Mexico and hung onto a piece of driftwood for over a week before they found him. Accourse, he was a big feller, good swimmer."

"And so was Judy, a good swimmer," Patricia said in her low voice. "That's why I just can't bring myself to believe—" She broke off, took the glass that Ward handed her, and touched it to her lips with obvious disinterest.

"How about planes and helicopters?" North boomed. "Did the police look all around here?"

"I believe they had a helicopter up the first morning," Barbara said. "Didn't they, Townley? I—well, I was so shocked by the whole thing that I didn't stir out of my room. I was *so* fond of Judy."

"Everybody was," Ward said quietly. "About the helicopter —yes, there was one, and a couple of planes besides all the boats."

High heels tapped on the pier's planking and another young

woman came hurrying toward the pavilion, her step buoyant, the pier lights casting a nimbus about her high-held head.

"Here I am, late as usual," she cried as she approached the group in the pavilion. "Sorry, but I got on the phone and you know how I am about telephones."

She came across the circle of deck chairs with her hand held out to Sue Anne Pendleton. "You must be Barbara's classmate that she's talked so much about," she said cordially. "I'm Gail Grafton." And added: "You're even prettier than Barbara said you were."

While the girl from Georgia sought something in answer to that neat remark, Gail Grafton turned and moved toward North, still standing in all his booted and sombreroed finery beside his chair. "And you must be Yahoo Gregory, right?" she asked.

"They been havin' trouble makin' a duplicate," Hugh confided and took the girl's hand. It was a strong handshake that Gail gave him, and as their fingers touched, the girl's fine eyes studied him, her mouth curved in a friendly smile.

"Did you really buy that hotel where the desk clerk snooted you?" she asked.

"Nope," North answered promptly. "Bought the property next door and opened up a penny arcade that runs twenty-four hours a day. Business at that high-class hotel ain't been so good lately, I hear."

There was a ripple of uneasy laughter about the circle, not joined in by Patricia. Gail cast Miss Forthier a glance (a strange blend of sympathy and exasperation) and then headed for the bar. Over her shoulder she asked: "Warm up anybody's cup while I'm up?"

Nobody needed a drink, Hugh concealing the fact that his glass was empty by spreading his oversized palm, and Gail helped herself. The G-2 colonel noticed two things: first, Gail poured a good four ounces of vodka into her glass and added only a dollop of quinine water, and, secondly, her long, blunt-ended fingers trembled slightly as she handled the mixing ingredients.

Why the slug and why the shakes? Does this pretty girl hit

*the sauce too hard or is she under the same strain that has
her old man jittery?*

Gail sauntered back toward the semicircle of chairs and
dropped into one next to Townley Ward. She was a handsome
girl, bigger of frame than the average, twenty-five by her
dossier, with dark hair and clean, lithe lines, her mother's
daughter, not her father's. Although trying not to let first im-
pressions steer him, Hugh detected an air of defiance in her
attitude, a reined-in resentment toward some member of this
group. Her stepmother? Quite probably; it was pretty definite
that Gail Grafton had not approved of her father's romance
with Ted Winslow's beautiful young wife. Or was Gail on the
outs with Townley Ward—or did Patricia Forthier's presence
annoy her?

The new arrival applied herself to her drink, then looked
about. "Where's Terry?" she asked. "I thought he was down
here with the rest of you."

"Haven't seen him since dinner," Townley Ward said idly.
"Maybe he went over to St. George's."

"I think he mentioned something about an early-morning
fishing trip," Barbara explained. "Perhaps he's gone to bed."
She turned toward North. "My brother, Terry James," she
explained.

"I'm dyin' to see Terry," Sue Anne Pendleton offered. "He's
one of the cutest boys I know."

North breathed a silent grunt. Terry James was cute, all
right, if his reputation half did him justice. Since prep-school
days, Terry James had kept his family busy extricating him
from one jam after another and now, at twenty-seven, he
seemed to have lost none of his skill at getting involved in
superscrapes. These involvements had included three brief
marriages, each costing a sizable chunk of the James fortune
to fix, and innumerable attachments unblessed by marriage
vows but attended by headlines.

"A screwball," Hugh's General had said bluntly. "Not especially dangerous except for the fact that he always needs
money. His family keeps him on an allowance he considers
ridiculous, and these high-flying young men who are per-

petually broke sometimes hire themselves out in the damnedest jobs—which might include Commie connections, so keep
an eye on Master James."

"Was there something you wanted to see Terry about, Gail
dear?" Barbara Grafton was asking, almost too sweetly.

Gail shook her lovely head. "No, I just wondered where he
was, that's all."

"You weren't afraid he might have been looking in on your
little tête-à-tête with Stan Gibbons, were you, darling?"

Gail swung toward her stepmother so quickly that her dark
hair swished with the motion. "What do you mean, tête-à-
tête?"

Barbara sipped her drink, her rings glittering in the light.
"Oh, Gail, don't be so naïve. Everybody on Plunder Island
knows Stan Gibbons brought his ketch into Hidden Bay this
afternoon. Did you think he could come here without one of
the servants seeing him and reporting to me?"

North was able to catch Gail's flush, even in this subdued
light. "It's not very nice to know I'm being spied on," the
girl said, her voice hurt.

"Such an ugly term, spied on," Barbara retorted, still calmly. "Your father prefers to think you're being protected from
your girlish infatuation. I'm inclined to agree with him—I take
a dim view of fortune-hunting nobodies myself."

"Now, see here—" Gail began hotly, but Townley Ward
stepped in.

"Hold it, hold it," he cried. "Let's sheathe the claws, girls,
and enjoy this beautiful night. All family squabbles are here-
by postponed until after Mr. Gregory and Sir George leave—
then you can go at it tooth and nail."

"Sir George?" Hugh North asked. "Who's Sir George?"

"Sir George Pakenham," Ward explained. "He's due tomorrow to sit in on our little conference. Didn't Wes tell you
about him?"

"Oh, the dook," North said. "Yeah, over the phone he said
somethin' about some Englishman buyin' chips for this game.
Does he wear a monocle and all that sort of rot, hey?"

"I think," Barbara Grafton murmured, "that you've got a surprise coming when you meet Sir George, Mr. Gregory."

"Call me Yahoo," North urged. "Hell, we're old friends by now. And not meanin' to butt in on family fights—not much, anyway—but what's wrong with this Stan Gibbons feller that your pa won't let him come to the house and set at the table, Miss Gail?"

"Well, really—" Townley Ward began but this time it was Gail who interrupted him.

"Nothing's wrong with Stan, Yahoo," she said earnestly. "It's just that he hasn't got very much money—"

"And absolutely no prospects of any unless he marries you," Barbara put in.

Gail shot her stepmother a glance that almost hissed through the night air but kept on determinedly. "Stan just hasn't made the almighty dollar his god, that's all," she told North. "He's going to be a great ichthyologist some day."

"Ichthy-what?" Hugh goggled.

"Ichthyologist," Gail repeated. "The study of marine life. Stan's already known in his field for his photography and in a few years he'll be at the top, given a break."

"Given a break and an heiress for a wife," Barbara Grafton murmured.

Gail's eyes were hot and the hand holding her glass trembled. "You're so—so mean!" she cried. "Honestly, Barbara, I don't know why you're so determined to break things up between Stan and me. Goodness knows *you're* in no position to criticize anybody after the way—"

"Now, that really is enough," Townley Ward said firmly as he got out of his chair. "We're all forgetting that Miss Forthier is here."

Silence clapped itself over the group in their guilty realization of the fact that a bereaved girl was being subjected to the unpleasantness of a family quarrel. It was Hugh North who broke the silence by yawning mightily, throwing his long arms out in a massive stretch.

"Well, hell," he said, "if there ain't goin' to be any more

excitement, I might as well go on up to bed. Got some things to go over with my secretary, anyway, before I sack in."

He got out of his chair, weaved just a tiny fraction, and then turned toward the shore end of the pier. "Nobody get up," he ordered. "I can find my own way if somebody'll tell me what room I been put in."

"It's at the end of the west wing," Barbara Grafton said, pointing a long-nailed finger toward one end of the sprawling house, Freebooter's Hall. "If you don't see Wesley, who seems to have been detoured somewhere, the butler will show you to your rooms, Mr. Gregory."

"You ain't ever gonna call me Yahoo, are you?" North asked wistfully.

Before the mistress of Freebooter's Hall could frame a response, Hugh headed out of the pavilion. He stopped as Patricia Forthier called after him. "I'll go up with you, Mr. Gregory," she said.

The colonel turned back to see the long-faced woman confronting Barbara. "Mrs. Grafton, if you'll put up with me I'd like to stay on," she said earnestly. "Just in case—well—"

"Of course," Barbara said tonelessly. "As long as you like, my dear." There was no warmth in her voice; even an obtuse person could have caught the note of inhospitality.

Gail Grafton added a word in a much more sympathetic tone. "It's not a question of putting up with you, Patricia— you mustn't think that. Please don't dream of leaving for at least a week—longer, if you can put up with *us.*"

Patricia nodded her thanks to Gail and walked out of the pavilion to join North. For once, Hugh kept Yahoo's stridency muted; this girl was joining him for a purpose unless he was very wrong.

They walked up the pier in silence until they were almost at the land end. Then the woman spoke, her voice little more than a husky murmur. "Mr. Yahoo," she said, "I—will you be my friend? I need one badly."

"Why sure, ma'am," the colonel said, his voice gentled so it would reach no listening ears at the pavilion. "Be proud to. But the folks back there seemed friendly enough."

"They're not," Patricia Forthier said decisively. "Oh, Gail might be—or maybe she's just pretending. Maybe she's playing their game with them."

"Game, ma'am?"

"Yes, an evil, cruel game." The slender girl turned her long, unsmiling face toward North. "They're *afraid*," she went on. "And I think I know why they're afraid. My sister—I'm almost sure my sister was murdered."

3.

[1]

HUGH'S HEART gave a great bound but he stayed in character. One hand went up to tilt back the wide sombrero as he stopped in his tracks, peered down at the girl.

"You know what you're sayin'?" he asked.

Patricia nodded. "Oh yes, I know," she said bitterly.

"And you're accusin' one of these people of bein' a killer?"

The girl hesitated, then hedged. "I'm *almost* sure Judy was murdered," she said. "She was such a good swimmer that it's almost impossible she could drown."

"Best swimmers in the world can get cramps or heart attacks or somethin'," North said. "Knew a feller once that—"

"She wouldn't, not Judy," Patricia interrupted. "You didn't know her. She's been swimming all her life, and in the ocean; she wouldn't go in the water if she was sick or—or tight, like they say she was. She knew how dangerous it could be."

"Well, everybody makes a slip once in a while; maybe it was her turn," North said, and hastened to add: "Don't think I'm brushin' you off, Miss Forthier. If you need a friend like you say you do, I'm your man, but I don't want you to go off half cocked. I—"

He stopped as there was the sound of footsteps on the shell walk leading down from Freebooter's Hall to the pier.

"When can I talk to you where we can be private?" he asked swiftly.

Patricia looked up at him, hesitant, dubious.

"I'm your friend, remember?" North urged.

"All right. My room, the last in the east wing, the one Judy used to have. Not too soon. In about—say three o'clock. They all ought to be asleep by then."

"I'll be there," Hugh said and raised his voice to hail the approaching dim figure. "Hey, that you, Grafton?"

Wesley Grafton's answering voice was faintly slurred, and Hugh North blessed the fact that his host had kept on with his drinking after leaving the pier. "Uh-huh," Grafton said as he came up to the couple. "Had some things to tend to. You turning in already, Yahoo?"

"I got the yawns and there's a mess of things to be signed that Kenny's been workin' on," the colonel explained. "Miss Forthier, here, she's tired, too, so we came along up."

"I'll show you your room," Grafton said, ignoring Patricia.

"Ain't no need to do that," the colonel protested. "They're waitin' for you on the dock."

"Let'm wait," Grafton said with a sweeping gesture that nearly carried him off balance. "This way." His step was not staggering; it was the rigidly controlled walk of a man who knows he has had too much to drink and is determined not to let anyone else know it.

Patricia Forthier murmured something and left. North followed his host, telling himself that if Barbara Grafton had been uncordial, her husband was downright rude to the sister of the missing Judy Forthier—if Patricia was a sister.

"We put you in the west wing," Grafton was saying. "Off by yourself there and it's quiet. Sleep as late as you like— Pakenham won't be here 'til noon or thereabouts."

"Hell, podner, I can't keep my eyes closed after it gets light," North rumbled. "Spent too many years gettin' up and beddin' down with the sun."

The two men entered the house, a place of beautifully furnished, high-ceilinged rooms through which the night breeze coursed ceaselessly. They walked through an enormous living room outfitted with the rattan and bamboo furniture peculiar to these islands. At the end of the drawing room, a comparatively narrow corridor stretched in each direction, the hallway off which the sleeping apartments opened.

Patricia Forthier had preceded them into the house and now North saw her, halfway down the east-wing hall. He looked after the woman, then said to Grafton: "That girl sure is shook up about her sister, Wes. Damn shame."

The millionaire cast a murky look at the hurrying figure of Patricia Forthier. "Yeah," he said. "I wish she'd—well, I don't suppose it's her fault, but she gets on my nerves with her eternal weeping and those reproachful looks. As though she blamed us for what happened to her sister. My God, it wasn't our fault the girl went swimming in the middle of the night, was it?"

"Damn shame," North said again, and followed Grafton down the·long, dimly lit corridor of the west wing. The G-2 colonel got an idea of the great expanse of this house as he trailed his host. The darkness had prevented more than a guess at the size of Freebooter's Hall from the outside but now North realized that by the stretch of this west wing, Grafton's Bermuda residence must be a tropical mansion. The G-2 agent counted ten widely spaced doors on his way down the hall, each far enough from its neighbor to indicate a bedroom, sitting room, and bath suite.

"Here we are," the millionaire said as he came to the last door in the wing. "Hope you find it comfortable." He tried the knob and found the door locked, looked surprised. "Who could've—oh, forgot your secretary," he said, and raised his knuckles to rap.

Kenny Trotter opened up immediately and Grafton stood aside to let Hugh into the room, then followed his guest inside. *Come for a look-around, little man, or do you just want another drink?*

"Hi, Kenny-boy," the G-2 colonel said. "You finish up that work I told you to take care of?"

"Most of it, sir," Trotter replied, his voice precise. "That

Garrabrandt contract had that clause in it, just as you suspected, sir."

"Told you so," North grunted, grinning.

And Wesley C. Grafton did not know, would never know, that Lieutenant Trotter had just said to Colonel North: "This room is bugged."

Hugh headed for the liquor cabinet set in a corner of the small, neat sitting room (with the fleeting thought that he doubtless would find some kind of drink dispenser in the bath), splashed bourbon into a glass, and turned to Grafton with the bottle in his hand. "Join me in a nightcap?" he asked.

"Don't mind if I do. Scotch, please."

The colonel shook his head reprovingly. "When you goin' to learn to swaller a man-sized likker?" he asked. "Save your Scotch for the dook, what's-his-name, Pakenham." He reached for the bottle of Grant's and tossed a dismissal at Kenny.

"Hit the sack, boy. Busy day tomorrow so don't go tomcattin' down at the village."

Kenny looked shocked. "Village, sir? I don't think there's one on this island, is there?"

"Hell, you'd swim through a storm at sea to get to a gal; don't tell me," Hugh laughed. "I saw you givin' that pretty Sue Anne Pendleton the eye."

"Oh, sir," Kenny Trotter protested, "you'll give Mr. Grafton the wrong idea about me."

Wesley Grafton took his drink and swallowed thirstily. "Take my advice and leave Sue Anne alone, both of you," he counseled. "She may look like an ordinary dizzy blonde but she's poison." He swigged again. "I didn't want her down here but Barbara insisted," he confided when he could speak again. "My wife feels sorry for her. The Pendletons lost all their money a while back and Sue Anne's been mooching on her old friends ever since."

"What way is she poison?" North asked.

"To men," Grafton said succinctly. "She gobbles 'em. Never gets enough of 'em. Somethin' wrong with her glands, I guess —anyway, she's not much better than a blue-blooded tramp."

North grinned more widely. "Hear that, Kenny-boy? Hands

off. I don't want my secretary goin' around all pooped out, not 'til this deal's signed, sealed, and delivered, anyhow. Go along and get your sleep."

Trotter gave a slight bow and went through the connecting door into his bedroom. North waited until the door closed and then asked Grafton: "Speakin' of the deal, what about it? You said on the phone and in the letter your man brought me that there was a lot of dough to be picked up on a long-term investment—what's the lowdown?"

Grafton swallowed a mouthful of Scotch. "We'd better wait 'til tomorrow," he suggested. "We're both tired and we've had a few drinks. I can tell you that—well, it's a big thing."

"Hell, I wouldn't be here if I didn't think it was big," North said. "Gimme something more than that. You fellers makin' up a syndicate, is that it?"

"In a manner of speaking," Grafton nodded. "I've got the way paved for us to get hold of some interests in a Central American country. Tin, bauxite, oil—the whole business. I've worked a long time to set this thing up and they're not going to take it away—well, I've got a sweetheart of a proposition for you, Yahoo."

"What Central American country you speakin' of?" North asked bluntly.

Wesley Grafton, however, was not saying, not within range of the bug that Kenny Trotter had discovered and which undoubtedly had a listener at the other end of the line. *The missing Terry James?* Grafton scowled, shook his head.

"Too early to tell you that," he said. "Wait'll you hear some of the details, the requirements. Wait'll tomorrow when we get down to cases." He nodded his head toward the connecting door Kenny had used. "Is your secretary dependable?" he asked. "I'd hate to have any of the details of this deal get out."

"Hell, yes," North replied. "Do you think I'd have anybody around me I couldn't trust? I got as much confidential stuff as you have to work with—maybe more."

Grafton held up a placating hand. "Just wanted to be sure,"

he said. "I had a secretary once who was working for the opposition, it turned out. Cost me a fortune."

"Wasn't that Forthier gal who drowned, I hope," Hugh North said, and sloshed more bourbon down the hatch. When he looked at Wesley Grafton again he found the millionaire's bloodshot eyes fixed upon him intently.

"Why'd you say that?" demanded the master of Freebooter's Hall.

North shrugged his wide shoulders. "Just askin', like you were," he said calmly. "Be funny, though, if you did find out Judy Forthier was pullin' a fast one and then she drowned right after that—accidentally."

"That's a hell of a thing to say," Grafton growled.

"My, my, ain't you the touchy one, though?" the false Yahoo Gregory scoffed. "Don't tell me you never heard of such things bein' done, gettin' rid of somebody that might bollix up a deal—gettin' rid of 'em permanently. I'd hate to think of all the people that met up with accidents in my game, just because they were tryin' to do some sharpshootin'. But maybe my game's a little rougher than yours, Grafton. Maybe you just slap people on the wrist when you find they've been double-crossin' you."

"No," Wesley Grafton said after a moment's hesitation. "No, we play rough, too. But that wasn't the case with Miss Forthier. Not with Judy."

He went to the bar to replenish his drink and North's eyes were speculative as they regarded his back. "You sort of had a thing goin' with Judy Forthier, didn't you, podner?" the G-2 man asked.

Grafton swung about violently. "No!" he cried. "I didn't—of course not! Dammit, I resent such a suggestion, Gregory!"

How can you afford to resent it? Hugh stiffened his face. "Now don't get up on no high horse with me," he warned. "I know you're a big wheel and high society and all that but you're no plaster saint, Grafton; you wouldn't sneeze at a chance to make a little time with a good-lookin' secretary, no more than I would, so don't try to pull that resent-the-suggestion stuff with me."

For a moment it seemed as though Wesley Grafton might really blast, tell off this crude Westerner who was his guest at Freebooter's Hall. If he had, North was prepared to backtrack hastily. He could not afford to be dealt out of the conference on the morrow, and he had his rough-hewn apologies all prepared while he waited for Grafton's next move. The millionaire wrestled with his anger for a moment and then put on a ghastly grin—ghastly because it must have cost him a lot in self-respect.

"I can see you're a man of the world, eh, Yahoo?" he asked. "But for God's sake, don't let my wife ever find out. She'd walk out on me. Very puritanical, my wife."

North pursued his advantage. "I won't spill a word," he promised, "but if I was you I'd put up a better front than you have so far. I mean when we was comin' over on the boat and Sue Anne made that crack about maybe it wasn't safe here —hell, anybody could see that shook you up down to your bootheels. And what about the kid drownin'? Anything wrong with it?"

"Of course not."

"The law is satisfied it was an accident? No chance of any trouble there? I want to know because Yahoo Gregory ain't gettin' mixed up in any deal where there's a chance the cops might walk in askin' questions about a missin' girl. I'll take my chances at matchin' wits with the government, even the Internal Revenue boys, on business deals but I don't want any cop that's lookin' for headlines to put me over the jumps about a gal I never even met."

"You haven't anything to worry about," Grafton insisted. "I tell you Inspector Boyd's written the case off as an accident."

"How much did you pay him?" North asked matter-of-factly.

Grafton shook his head. "You don't know the Bermuda police," he said, "and especially Boyd. He won't even take a drink or a cigar. No, it's on the level. The police think she drowned while swimming, half crocked."

"They *think* so, do they?" North grunted. "Well, what's the real scoop, then? And don't try to sell me the same story you gave the cops. I ain't buyin' that."

It was a stroke that looked bolder on its surface than it really was. Hugh North actually was prepared to have Grafton stick to the accidental drowning story and the G-2 colonel was ready to accept it, finally, possibly because Grafton, at least, thought it was the true story. However, according to Hugh's thinking there was nothing to be lost by the shot in the dark; he had made similar shots in the past that had brought a resounding bong from the hidden bull's-eye's gong.

He scored an immediate hit this time, although not a bull's-eye. Grafton's liquor-reddened eyes flitted to the valances above one of the windows and their venetian blinds.

So that's where your bug is, eh? And you hate like hell to have your ear hear the straight story. Which proves there is another story.

"Come on," he prodded. "I got to be sure you're levelin' with me all the way, Grafton. You want me to sit in on your deal, you'd better gimme the real dope about Judy Forthier."

He witnessed an agonizing struggle within Wesley Grafton before the millionaire silently raised a finger and beckoned North to follow him. The G-2 colonel trailed the master of Freebooter's Hall into the gleaming bathroom beyond the bedroom and closed the door behind him.

"What in hell?" Hugh asked, although he knew; there was no bug here.

"Just want to be sure we can't be overheard," Grafton explained. "I—maybe I'm making a mistake telling you, Yahoo."

"If you don't trust me, okay; we'll call off the deal and I'll be on my way in the mornin'," the colonel said grimly.

Silently, he said: *You need me real bad, don't you?*

"Of course I trust you," Grafton said nervously. "Otherwise I'd never have brought you into the syndicate. The others —but never mind. What I'm going to tell you is a touchy thing, that's all. A damned touchy thing."

North waited, his face expressionless, shaded by the brim of the ever-present sombrero. Grafton leaned so close that the colonel caught the redolence of the millionaire's Scotch.

"All right," Wesley Grafton whispered, "this is the real story. Judy Forthier killed herself, poor child."

[2]

North felt his pulses hammer in his ears. First accident, now suicide—and was murder the real answer?

"What happened?" he asked Grafton.

The pudgy millionaire wiped the back of his hand across his sweating forehead. "She—she got in trouble," he explained, still in that hushed whisper. "She liked a good time, Judy did, and she wasn't much of a drinker—nothing to compete with this crowd. I suppose she was tight the night she—well, when she got herself pregnant."

"You?" North asked stonily.

Grafton's face was distorted by a spasm. Fear? Resentment? "No, I swear it," he said. "It was that damned Stan Gibbons, the man who's always hanging around my daughter, Gail."

"The fish expert?"

Grafton nodded, his face lined and weighted now, his eyes brooding. "That skunk," he said. "I saw him fooling around with Judy when Gail wasn't looking and I warned her but she wouldn't listen. She came to me when—when she found out she was caught. Begged me to find a doctor for her but I wouldn't; I draw the line at that. I told her I'd look out for her all the way and I thought she cheered up a little, accepted the bad break, but she didn't."

"What did Gibbons have to say about it?" Hugh asked.

"Judy begged me not to go to him. Said she—she told him and he laughed at her, told her it was a case of which tooth of the buzz saw and she—well, she was in a hell of a fix. You see, there *had* been others, even though she was sure Gibbons was the man."

This was a Counterintelligence agent?

"So what happened?" Hugh asked.

"It was the way I told you, up to a point. Judy did slip away from that party, and somebody heard her say she might take a swim to clear her head. It was as though the poor kid wanted to make sure there'd be no scandal."

"Well, how d'you know—"

"She left a note," Grafton broke in, his voice tormented. "I found it in my desk. I've got it here with me."

He fumbled in his hip pocket, extracted a wallet, and took from it a folded sheet of notepaper which he handed to North. Hugh read: *I can't go through with it. Forgive me. This is the best way. Good-by and thank you for your kindness.* The note was signed by initials, *J.F.*

The G-2 colonel raised a hand to scratch the back of his reddened neck, his lips pursed doubtfully. "This looks okay to me," he said slowly. "I suppose it's her handwritin'."

Grafton's glare was venomous. "Of course. I'd know my own secretary's handwriting, wouldn't I? What are you getting at? This proves it was suicide, doesn't it?"

"Why, sure, Wes," Hugh North said. And his mind protested: *The hell it does.*

When Wesley Grafton finally left—after another nightcap and more assurances to Yahoo Gregory that there would be no trouble with the police, no chance of their discovering that Judy had committed suicide, Hugh North went about the business of undressing, showering noisily, and climbing into the pajamas that Kenny had laid out for him. He dawdled at his work, giving the ear that listened in on that bug several choruses of some nameless tune, trolled discordantly, as he padded back and forth across the big bedroom. At length he snapped off all the lights except one on a night table, climbed into the big, deep bed, folded his hands across his chest, and waited.

Ten minutes passed before the connecting door swung open and the red dot of a cigarette heralded the approach of Kenny Trotter, attaché case in hand. Unbidden by word or gesture from the man in the bed, the lieutenant snubbed out his cigarette, lowered the case to a chair, and extracted from it an instrument that might have been an oversized hypodermic needle, its tube filled with a colorless liquid.

As silent as a shadow, Kenny took a chair over to a spot beneath the valance Grafton had glanced at, climbed up, and stretched his lean length to touch the cleverly concealed connecting wires of the tiny bug with the needle's tip. Deftly, the colonel's aide injected a dose of what G-2 agents termed "silencer" into the insulated wire. Then he climbed down.

Kenny Trotter had used one of the most priceless Mickey Finns ever to have come out of G-2's own laboratories. It was a preparation designed to counteract the increasingly popular use of listening devices. The syringe's fluid carried properties that immediately, effectively, and permanently ruined the wires as conductors without damaging the insulation in the least, by stain or any other giveaway mark. An experienced electrician or electronics man could be driven stark, staring mad by frustration in trying unsuccessfully to find out what had gone wrong with that bug. Hugh North and other G-2 agents had found the new discovery valuable in silencing listening devices planted on them without giving the opposition any real reason to suspect that they, the G-2 men, were onto the game.

Lying back on his pillow, Hugh mentally counted to ten slowly and then said: "I take it you found only one bug."

"Just that one, *mon colonel*," Kenny nodded. "No pictures that aren't pictures or mirrors with two-way vision, either."

"Were you able to plant anything of ours?"

Kenny shook his head ruefully. "No, except a connecting line between your room and mine. I managed to find out where everybody sleeps in this mink-lined squirrel cage, but our bugs will have to wait. And what do you think of Grafton's story about Judy committing suicide because she was *enceinte?*"

North shrugged. "Not much," he grunted. "Judy might have used her bed talents in line of duty, but I hardly think State would send out a girl who'd be so careless as to get caught—and by an ichthyologist, at that."

Kenny seated himself on the side of the bed and lit another cigarette, blew smoke toward the ceiling. "If Judy wasn't pregnant then she didn't commit suicide, which means she was murdered," he offered.

"Her sister Patricia says she's almost sure she was—if Patricia really is her sister," North said. "I talked with her for a couple of minutes and while she bore down heavy on Judy being a good swimmer, there was something else for her to base her suspicions on, I think. I'm seeing her at three o'clock in her room, for further details."

Kenny gave a long, low whistle. "Fast worker, this guy North," he said.

"You haven't seen the stern Patricia Forthier," North grumbled. "Now if it was Sue Anne Pendleton . . . " He reached out to the bedside lamp and snapped it off for the benefit of whoever might be watching the windows. "Have you found out anything, Kenny?"

"Not much," Trotter admitted. "Item One: our rooms were bugged—I've taken care of that. Two: the butler, a guy named Blair, was Barbara Grafton's servant when she was Barbara Winslow. He won't talk, too stuffed-shirt. Three: Creepy, that boatman, runs the native servants with an iron hand. They're scared of him—something to do with the local brand of voodoo."

"Gombey," North supplied.

"Well, whatever it is, our Creepy seems to be a big wheel in the organization."

"How did you find this out?" Hugh asked.

"I got hungry," Kenny explained. "Wandered around until I found the kitchen. It's simple enough for somebody in my position; they consider secretaries as hired hands around here, and it's easy to join the backstairs club."

"And people were still up in the kitchen?"

"Sure. I don't know whether Grafton runs his servant staff in shifts or these natives just like to stay up late; anyway, there was a cook, a couple of housemaids, and a yardman back there drinking coffee and talking in an Oxford accent. Honest, these people are harder to understand than the Chinese until you get the swing of it. I got in good right away, incidentally, by making you out all kinds of an s.o.b."

"Well, thanks," Hugh murmured dryly.

"It was expected," Kenny grinned. "No man is a hero, et cetera, et cetera, and these servants have become accustomed to assorted brands of stinkers visiting here as Grafton's house guests. I knew you'd want to be accepted as just another rich no-good so I really laid it on."

"To what result, aside from your own nice warm feeling?"

"Well, we compared heels and I found out that of all the heels at Freebooter's Hall, Barbara's brother, Terry James, heads the list. He's a maid-chaser par excellence. I tried to get the maids to show me their bruises but they wouldn't."

"I'm looking forward to meeting that young man, James," Hugh said. "We can't throw Grafton's suicide story out the window without looking into it, and if Judy Forthier *was* in trouble, Terry James might have been the one responsible. Grafton hates Gibbons and he might be shielding his brother-in-law and—"

"Not a chance, from what the servants say," Trotter broke in. "They say Grafton would like nothing better than to see Terry James gone, but forever."

"Not if it would mean letting Barbara get away," Hugh said.

"You think he's got it big for Barbara?"

"Definitely. I don't know how Grafton got her but I think he realizes he got a prize in anybody's book. Money, beauty, and family."

"And so he shows how proud he is by getting all slopped up?" Kenny asked.

Hugh frowned, shook his head. "I'm not sure if the liquoring-up is a regular thing or if it's brought on by this Forthier incident," he said. "And Barbara doesn't seem to be such a bad hand with the bottle, herself. Maybe these people in this stratum of society are all heavy drinkers."

"I wouldn't know," Trotter murmured.

"I was just thinking," North began. "If—"

He broke off as he and Kenny tensed, shocked out of speech by the hammer of a gun, behind Freebooter's Hall but close by.

[3]

Both men reacted more or less instinctively. While Hugh snapped on his light, jumped into the ludicrously tight pants and boots that Yahoo Gregory affected, Kenny Trotter ran for his bedroom and slipped on a pair of slacks and dressing gown. Hugh, in the character of Yahoo, spurned a similar robe and the gun he carried as he preceded Kenny out into the hall was a massive, pearl-handled .45, not the snub-nosed .38 that he regularly used. The sombrero, be it added, was firmly in place.

There were no cries or shouts, no commotion at all, as they burst out into the hall. Unless everybody was still down on the pier, Freebooter's Hall seemed to be taking the gunshot very calmly indeed.

North headed for the main hall, and as he was skidding around the corner on his high heels he came face to face with a comely dark-skinned housemaid. The girl stared at his broad, bare torso, then looked past him at Trotter and smiled, her teeth dazzling white.

"You hear de shot?" she asked in her low, inimitable island accent. "Don' worry; it's only Creepy after de rats."

"Rats?" North bellowed, back in character. "Whaddaya mean?"

The maid pointed toward the rear of the house. "De rats from de castle come stealin' over in de night," she explained musically, "and Creepy, he shoot 'em with de gun. He never miss."

"I gotta see this," Hugh said. "How do we get out there?"

The maid directed the colonel and his aide to a door that opened onto a wide, flagged *lanai*. Some distance away bobbed a flashlight. "Dere's Creepy," the girl said, and giggled deliciously. "Better make sure he don' t'ink you're de rat, sar," she said. "Better halloo to Creepy before you get in de range of de gun."

"Good advice," Yahoo nodded and reached into the tight

pants, extracted a ten-dollar bill. "Here's somethin' for your trouble."

Astonishingly, the girl shook her head. "No thank you, sar," she said pleasantly. "Creepy, he don' like for us to take tips, sar."

"Hooey," North blared. "You'll take 'em from me. Here." As the girl still protested, the man in the sombrero tucked the bill against the warm skin under the neckline of the prim but well-curved uniform and stalked off toward the flashlight, ignoring the maid's protests.

"Ten dollars, *mon colonel?*" Kenny Trotter breathed at Hugh's side.

"Yahoo's not cheap," North muttered out of the corner of his mouth. He raised his voice in a shout, "Hey, Creepy, it's me, Yahoo Gregory. You get that rat?"

There was a brief silence, and then the boat captain's reply. "Always get de rat, sar. Never miss."

The two men came into the circle of light cast by Creepy's torch and followed the direction pointed by Creepy's forefinger to see a rat as big as a puppy lying on the grass border of a flower bed. North stared and despite himself he felt a slight shiver ripple up his spine; he once had had a very rugged time with rats in Korea.[*]

"They grow 'em big down here, don't they?" he asked.

"Dey all fat," Creepy agreed. "De castle, she full of 'em and dey come over to this island by some passage under de Pass that nobody ever found. Mr. Grafton tells me to shoot de ones that come here and I do. I got 'em scared—now only one comes once in a while where dey used to be lots of 'em."

"What d'you do, shine 'em with your flashlight?" North asked.

"Oh, no, sar. Don' use any light at all. Dey run from a light. I creep up on 'em without any light. Dat's why dey call me Creepy, sar."

"Well, I'll be damned," Hugh growled. "Man can see in the

[*]See *The China Sea Murders* (Pocket Books, Inc., 1959).

dark like a cat. Hey, that'd come in real handy sometimes, wouldn't it, Kenny-boy?"

"Yes, sir," Kenny said, and yawned.

North turned back to Creepy. "Tell me, you seen this Terry James, Mrs. Grafton's brother, around this evenin'?"

Creepy's black eyes suddenly went blank, and North knew he would never get any information from this man. "No, sar," the boat captain said. "You ask Mr. Grafton, he'll tell you where Mr. James is."

"Hell, I asked him already and he said he didn't know," North grumbled. "Well, how about this feller, Stan Gibbons, I hear about—did his boat sail out of Hidden Bay again or is it still there?"

"Mr. Gibbons, sar?" Creepy's voice was as vague as though he never had heard the name before.

"Yeah, Miss Gail's sweetie," North prompted.

That brought a result, and a startling one. Creepy's eyes blazed suddenly and the Pequot-Bermudian's mouth thinned to a narrow line. "You be careful how you talk about Miss Gail," the man snapped.

North was jolted by the boatman's sudden and complete switch from the role of respectful servant. Hate spiked the dark man's voice and the hand that held the .22 rifle tightened in a spasmodic clutch.

Oh-ho, so that's it, eh? "Now, hold on," Hugh said aloud. "I didn't mean anything wrong by that, Creepy. I just heard Miss Gail's goin' to marry Gibbons, that's all. If it sounded wrong, excuse it; I didn't mean it the wrong way."

Creepy relaxed slowly and the fierce light in his eyes dimmed. "I'm sorry, sar," he said and walked to the rat, picked it up by its tail as North repressed a shudder. "I have work to do," the skipper of *Amphitrite* said simply, and walked away.

North stared after the slight, wiry figure in the white ducks and yachting cap. "He's got it bad," he murmured to Kenny Trotter.

"Oh, but all very proper," the aide muttered back. "I could have told you; it's common knowledge in the kitchen. Creepy adores Gail Grafton but in the reverent goddess-and-worshiper way, so don't get any wrong ideas."

"I couldn't," Hugh said, "not after having met Gail Grafton. She doesn't look the type who'd play booey-in-the-bushes with the hired help. Let's go back and try to get some rest. I've got that date at three and it's"—he checked his wrist watch—"one-thirty now."

Back in his room, North stretched himself on his bed, his arms behind his head, looking up at the ceiling while Kenny dropped into a chair across the room.

"Tomorrow," the G-2 colonel said, "I'd like you to scout around and get enough idea of this place to make me a floor plan. I might not need it but—"

"Already done, *mon colonel*," Trotter interrupted. "Actually, of course, I got the information to find out where the fair Sue Anne was bedded down. I'll get the floor plan."

He was back in a moment with a rough sketch of the layout of Freebooter's Hall. "Here's where you're going at three o'clock, here at the end of the east wing. Next door is Sue Anne and then comes the big master suite, Grafton and Mrs. G. Separate bedrooms with a dressing room between—not very cozy, I must say. Next, coming west, is Terry James' room, then Gail's, with this one between them empty. Here's the main hallway and then our wing, all empty except for the first suite, Townley Ward's, and ours. Pakenham is going into the rooms next to Ward's when he gets here. We're off by ourselves in left field—obviously so you won't contaminate the others."

North studied the sketch and nodded approval. "Fine," he said, "only the next time, give me an idea of what kind of cover I can expect outside, going from here to the end of the opposite wing."

"That's gratitude," Trotter groaned. "Here I work my fingers to the bone and—did you say outside? You mean you're going out into the night where lurks a rifleman who can see in the dark, sahib?"

"I'd have one hell of a job explaining why I was tramping

around in my fancy boots in the wrong wing if somebody popped out and asked me, wouldn't I?"

"You could tell 'em you're looking for the little boys' room," Kenny grinned. "Seriously, though, be careful of Creepy. He might think you were disrespectful to the great white goddess, Gail, and have you on his Gombey list. From what I hear, that's bad."

"What did the backstairs say about Creepy's Gombey connections?" North asked.

"That's one thing they don't say much about. I gather that discussing Gombey with a white man is taboo. But I did get the impression that what Creepy says goes in the Gombey local and in this household, too. For all you know, you may have doomed that little maid to death on the sacrificial altar by stuffing ten dollar bills down her buzzum. Creepy's rule is no tips, she told you."

North nodded and yawned, tilting the sombrero down over his face. His muffled voice came through the white felt. "Speaking of buzzums, leave Sue Anne Pendleton alone. You heard Grafton say she's a man-eater."

"I heard," Kenny grinned. "And how do you think she'd prefer me, medium rare or well done?"

The hands of North's watch crawled around the dial to a quarter of three and the G-2 colonel left his room to pay his call on Patricia Forthier.

He used the window instead of the door. The screen beyond the venetian blinds unlatched soundlessly, and the G-2 man eeled out of the opening with an absolute minimum of commotion. Aside from a pair of large, round spectacles, he was still Yahoo Gregory, although clad now in an all black outfit, from sombrero to boots, the whole tastefully decorated with silver-thread embroidery. He would have preferred a costume with no metallic strands to reflect light so gleamingly, but the advantages of a drab outfit were outweighed by the danger of being found outside of Yahoo's flamboyant character.

Hugh was fairly sure that Creepy had finished his rat hunt;

there had been only one other report, some distance to the south, since the one that had brought him and Kenny out of their rooms. The alcoholic intake of the group on the pier suggested that they should be asleep and snoring by now. If Freebooter's Hall ever slept, it should be sound at two-fifty-four on a still morning, and yet the colonel used all his skill as a stalker to slip silently from bush to bush, tree to tree, while he made the trip from the far end of the west wing to the end of the opposite wing.

He had taken half a dozen steps when he froze in his tracks, his heart clutched. *Something* stirred almost underfoot, something heavy, clumsy. As North waited, the *something* moved again—and again—in spaced, deliberate movements.

The G-2 officer wrinkled his brow; what in hell could that be? It was no rat, certainly no snake This thing was not exactly furtive, whatever it was, but its movements indicated a sort of secretive stealth.

Hugh's mind raced over a list of possibilities and found no answer to explain this eerie movement that headed away from him in regularly spaced sounds. He swallowed his qualms and took another step on his way. Another step—and there was that sound again, this time on his other side.

That settled it; he did not propose to be hemmed in, encircled by these mysterious skulkers. The colonel's left hand flashed to his hip pocket, the right hand withdrawing the pearl-handled gun from its armpit holster. North's left hand held a short, slender tube, innocent of nickel or any other reflecting metal, and this he put into action with the prod of a button.

The tube streaked out a shaft of light invisible to anyone who might be watching but as illuminating to Hugh North in his special spectacles as the beam from a powerful hand torch. It was G-2's most advanced development of "black light," the ray which kept itself hidden from all eyes not equipped with the compensating lenses such as Hugh North wore in the outsized spectacles.

The beam made a circle of invisible light on the dew-dampened grass, moved a foot to the right, back again and to the left—and Hugh repressed a laugh.

For there, owlishly staring up at him, was his furtive skulker, a giant toad.

The thing was as big as a small cat and glistening with damp. As North stared, half unbelieving, the giant gave a hop that carried it a good three feet, then another that took it out of the black ray's beam. North replaced his gun in its holster and swept the ground with his torch; the black light picked up three more toads in that relatively small expanse of rear lawn.

"Rats and toads," the G-2 colonel murmured beneath his breath. "All we need now are a couple of bats to have the ingredients of a witches' brew."

As though in answer to the thought, there were the whispers of bat wings passing close to the colonel's head. North ducked instinctively, then straightened with another laugh, this one directed at himself. He was getting nervy when he shied at a bat like a schoolgirl. No need to fear getting hit by one of those midnight travelers, not with their inborn radar systems.

He kept the torch on the ground, having no desire to step on one of those king-sized toads, as he moved along silently. From a marsh somewhere behind Freebooter's Hall came the squawk of some night bird; from the shore came the dull, rhythmic boom of a mild surf. The punk trees and palms that shrouded the back lawn with shadow patches shushed quietly in the gentle pre-dawn breeze. On the eastern horizon, a fingernail moon put in a belated appearance.

The G-2 operative made the east wing with no incident more noteworthy than having to sidestep half a dozen toads which refused to move out of his path. He found the window of the room Kenny Trotter had said was Patricia's and noted with satisfaction that it was well shadowed by a thick cycad palm; the colonel found it safe to stand beside the window for a long moment, listening for any untoward sounds. Satisfied that nobody except the toads was abroad in the immediate vicinity, he shone his light at the window.

Another break; the venetian blind was raised about a foot

above the sill, permitting North a chance to shine his black light into the room, sweep the enclosure with its beam. No time now for the safeguarding of Patricia's modesty, in any case, the girl would not know she had been spotlighted.

The bed was empty. The room was empty. The light coverlet was thrown back on the bed, but the pillow showed no indentation made by a head. The door to the bathroom stood open but Judy Forthier's self-styled sister was not there. Hugh's moving beam picked up a littered desk on which was a slender sheaf of papers, apparently letters, and a scattered pack of playing cards.

North frowned. Were Patricia Forthier's nerves so sound that she could play a game of solitaire while waiting for the visitor to whom she would explain her reasons for suspecting her sister's murder?

If, of course, Patricia really was Judy's sister and not a secret operative, an industrial spy, or a Red agent. It would be a good spot for either; as Judy's bereaved sister, Patricia naturally would have access to all the missing girl's effects and could go through them at her leisure. As a Counterintelligence agent, Judy Forthier should not have left any important information about—ever—but the best of agents sometimes slipped.

The colonel's pockets yielded a compact tool, no bigger than a small penknife, that would have been the underworld's most prized jewel if it ever had fallen into the hands of crooks. This was G-2's "can opener," with blades and hooks and flexible screw drivers capable of opening almost any locked or fastened object. It required North only a few seconds to loosen the screen fasteners *from the inside*, leaving only minute marks that would be invisible to all but the most powerful infrared inspection.

The screen disposed of, Colonel North slipped into Patricia's room and gave the place a thorough shakedown. It was the most logical next step that offered itself. The girl obviously had gone (or been lured) somewhere outside the house unless she, too, was sneaking around with a black-light torch; North had seen no sign of life astir in Freebooter's Hall during his trip the length of the island mansion. To pick up Patricia's trail now instead of taking advantage of her absence would be a wasted opportunity that might not come again. Hugh was uneasy about Patricia's whereabouts, but his job required that he give this room a going-over before anything else.

He moved to the desk and inspected the cards first, still using his black-light ray. The pasteboards had not been set in any solitaire layout known to Hugh; instead, they were sorted into piles with no special sequence of pips or suits.

The G-2 man picked up a couple of the topmost cards and found them nicked irregularly on one edge. He frowned, shook his head. *Not that old code!*

He moved on to the papers. The top sheet looked like the second page of a letter, written in a feminine hand. North's eyes narrowed as he breathed an ejaculation. This was almost the same handwriting as he had seen on the suicide note Grafton had shown him—*almost*, because while the resemblance was very close, close enough to be called identical by an untrained eye, there were tiny differences, little damning errors of copying, that yelled for the colonel's attention as he gave the page his expert perusal.

This, then, was Judy Forthier's real hand. The suicide note was a forgery, clever enough to be taken as genuine by most but not by a man as trained in spotting forgeries as Colonel Hugh North, Army Intelligence.

Hugh read the letter in his hand, and registered the exact wording, the punctuation, in his memory indelibly at first reading:

> *The whole beach party was aces-up! Quite the best I've ever been on. You'd have simply died to see Jack Quitman—he's a lawyer down here—taking off Queen Elizabeth reviewing the troops in a tight girdle. Around ten the moon came up and you should have seen Bunny King open up like a beautiful flower. Wow! What that girl can do with a nautch dance is nobody's business.*
>
> *Bunny's diamond was simply stunning and no wonder*

*she's happy. Jack's a doll, a member of the club from
way back! This time it's a real heart case, no "conven-
ience" thing.*

Hugh North's hand streaked out for the cards. So it *was* the
old code; that letter proved it. And what he knew now proved
that Judy Forthier had felt the hounds of danger and death
sniffing hot on her heels when she had written this.

[4]

The cards in a pocket of the ornate black and silver shirt,
North went on to the other letters on the desk. These proved
to be complete letters, all addressed to Judy, from people who
were not identified in the script, some women, some men.
These few bits of correspondence, apparently, were what Judy
had left behind her among her belongings, things that had
been turned over to Patricia, the bereaved sister.

Hugh swiftly scanned the letters, seeking the code that
might have been used in some of these, too, but found nothing. The desk drawers yielded nothing unusual. The spacious
closet was filled with two wardrobes, one obviously Patricia
Forthier's outfits and the other belonging to a much smaller
girl, Judy. Judy's gowns bore Hamilton labels that were simple enough to have come from an ultra-exclusive shop. Hugh
spared a moment to consider this fact: did Counterintelligence
give its agents as lavish expense accounts as G-2 had provided
him for the Yahoo Gregory masquerade or did somebody else's
checkbook carry the stubs representing these purchases? Perhaps Wesley Grafton's? Or Terry James'?

Rogers, the State Department man, had squirmed out of a
direct answer to how far Judy Forthier would play her agent's
game, to what extent she would use her feminine charms to
get the information she was after. Female undercover agents
dating back to Rahab, the harlot of Jericho who aided Joshua's
spies, had resorted to their most powerful means of persuasion
when the situation demanded; Hugh North could not find it

in him to damn Judy Forthier if she had found it necessary to become somebody's mistress to get information that might protect the security of her country.

And if she had done this, might she not have fallen in love with her intended informant-lover? Women fell in love, no matter if they were secret agents, and a woman in love was unpredictable. Hugh North was putting little credence in Wesley Grafton's suicide story but his experience had taught him that all angles, no matter how impossible they might seem, deserved consideration.

Patricia Forthier's clothes were unusual in that while all of them were of extremely fine quality and design, not one of them bore a label. North's inspection proved that at least four dresses had had their labels removed, so recently that the stitch holes still showed under a magnifying glass.

Nor, the colonel was to discover, was there a single item in all the articles he inspected that definitely identified its owner as Patricia Forthier, not a monogram, not a letter, or—in Patricia's purse found on a bureau—a driver's license, an "In Case of Accident" card or anything.

Frowning thoughtfully over this, Hugh went ahead with his shakedown. He found the bug that had been planted in the base of the bedside lamp, but it was impossible to tell whether Judy had doctored the wires as Kenny had done in the west-wing suite; the G-2 colonel found no "silencer" equipment here, but he knew Judy might have stashed such equipment in some hiding place outside the room.

North also found a recorder in the shape of a large compact in a dressing-table drawer. He stowed this with the playing cards, hoping the wire was jammed with facts but expecting the worst; an agent like Judy would hardly have kept a loaded recorder around; she would have forwarded it to her headquarters if it had been used.

That wound up the list of Hugh's discoveries. The bathroom yielded nothing upon relatively cursory examination. Patricia evidently had showered not too long before; drops still clung to the sides of the stall. There was no time to examine the toothpaste tube, sift the dusting-powder box, but

Hugh did take the few seconds needed to examine the huge tub sponge and found no hidden capsules there.

At length and after twenty action-packed minutes in Patricia's rooms, Hugh North straightened from an examination of all the heels of the shoes in their racks, satisfied that he had done all he could here at this time. Now to look for Patricia.

The indications were that Patricia Forthier had left this place in nightgown and dressing gown, her feet in slippers. The bedside chair had underthings flung over its back, and a pair of shoes that North remembered having seen on Patricia at the pier were beside the bed, obviously shucked as the girl prepared to retire.

Something, somebody, had caused this woman to leave her room in the middle of the night even though she said she believed the people about her included a murderer. A strange time and place for a stroll, North told himself grimly.

The G-2 agent left the room by the window, refastened the catches of the replaced screen, and hurried (but still carefully, carefully) back to his room in the west wing.

"She's missing," he told Kenny Trotter when he let himself back into the spacious room, via the window. "I went over the room and my first thought is that she's not Judy Forthier's sister. And Judy—or somebody—used the old card-edge code. If it was Judy, they caught up with her before she could deliver it."

Trotter whistled softly. "They must have been on top of her if she had to fall back on that old gimmick."

"Maybe it was a leave-behind message," North said darkly. "Maybe she knew it was her last message and she used the cards to let whoever followed her know what happened."

"Shall we get at the cards, then?"

"They'll have to wait," North snapped. "We have to find Patricia first—she may be in big trouble. I had to spend God's own time going over that room but it looked like my only chance if I stayed Yahoo Gregory. Come on, get dressed. We can say we heard a noise that might have been a scream. If the woman's okay, we heard an owl."

"Do they have owls in Bermuda?"

"A couple of rats fighting, then—those, they got."

Freebooter's Hall awoke at Yahoo Gregory's first bellow. Considering the heads that some of those sleeping people must have been carrying, North's howl must have been a voice from Hell, but they tumbled out of bed, Barbara Grafton first of all.

The door to Grafton's master suite opened and Barbara thrust out her head—lovely at a time when so few women were —before Hugh's shout had stopped echoing in the further reaches of the big house.

"For heaven's sake, what is it?" North's hostess demanded.

"We heard somethin'," Hugh explained. "Godawfullest noise you ever heard. Sounded like a banshee."

"Banshee?"

"Somebody gettin' choked or a couple of cats with their tails tied together," North embroidered.

"What's that? Screams?" Wesley Grafton reached around his wife and pulled the door open wider to stand in the doorway, an unlovely sight with his frizzed hair, baggy pajamas, raddled face. "You heard somebody scream?"

Hugh looked beyond Grafton and saw that Barbara wore only a diaphanous nightgown, its bosom raised by perfect breasts. As Yahoo Gregory he had to stare (no torturous task, certainly) and the dark-haired Barbara caught his leer, turned, and hurried out of sight. North reluctantly returned his eyes to Grafton.

"Yeah, screams," he said. "What kind of a place you got here, anyway? First, we have your boat captain shootin' up the joint—said he was after rats. Now we got screams at half-past three in the mornin'. Never a dull moment, hey, podner?"

As Grafton's lips moved soundlessly, Barbara returned into view, clad now in a dressing gown that was a gesture toward concealment, not much more. "You must have been dreaming," she told the colonel.

"Dreamin', hell! We both heard it. Like to scared Kenny-boy outta six years' growth."

"What's going on?" a new voice demanded. Hugh turned to meet Barbara's brother, Terry James, for the first time.

James was a crew-cut young man with a heavy tan and a powerful set of shoulders under the terry-cloth robe he wore. Despite his reputation for riotous living, his face showed no sign of dissipation; it was petulant, spoiled rotten, but it was neither lined nor baggy-eyed.

Ah, youth, North sighed inwardly. *There was a time when I, too, could live it up and not look like death warmed over the next day.*

Barbara's brother grinned up at the sombreroed man. "You're Yahoo Gregory," he said. "What gives, old boy?"

North returned the flip greeting sourly. Yahoo was supposed to be sensitive about two things, his baldness and his age. "Why, sonny," he drawled, "I dunno what gives but it sounded like somethin' that you'd maybe better hide under the bed about. It was a fearful screamin', that's what it was."

"Well, let's find out who screamed," James said, totally unsubdued. "Always investigate screams—first rule of the house. Never know but what the next scream might be yours, I always say."

"Oh, Terry, for goodness' sake," Barbara said in a disgusted voice. "Let's not be so bright at this time of day."

"Our Terry never forgets that he once shook hands with Noël Coward," Wesley Grafton said ponderously.

"What's all this about screams?" asked Townley Ward, coming up tightening the sash cord of his robe. "Who screamed?"

"That's what we intend to find out—if anybody really did," Barbara said. Of North she asked: "What direction did these noises come from?"

"Yonder," Hugh said, pointing down the hall toward Patricia's room. "At least I guess they did—hard to say."

Grafton scowled. "Sue Anne and Miss Forthier are down there. Let's see if they're all right."

"Of course they're all right," Townley Ward said. "What could happen to them? A bad dream, maybe, but nothing worse than that."

A door two apartments up from the Grafton suite outside

which the little group was congregated opened and Gail thrust out her tousled head. "For God's sake," she complained, "can't you hold your *Kaffeeklatsch* someplace else?"

"You okay, Gail?" Terry asked. "Somebody's been screaming around Freebooter's Hall."

"Didn't hear a thing," Gail muttered. She looked down at the wrist watch she wore. "Quarter of four," she said bitterly, and pulled in her head and closed the door with a bang.

"Come on," Wesley Grafton said, "let's make sure Sue Anne and that Forthier girl are all right." He stubbed down the hall toward the end of the wing, followed by North, Barbara, Terry, Townley Ward, and Kenny Trotter.

Grafton's first stop was at the door adjoining the apartment Hugh had just visited. The millionaire's knuckles were loud in the pre-dawn hush, and they brought a sleepy response from within.

"Are you all right, Sue Anne?" Barbara called.

There was a moment of puzzled hesitation. "All right? 'Course I'm all right. Shouldn't I be?"

Barbara explained: "Somebody thought they heard a scream. We're just checking up, dear. It's all right; go back to sleep."

"Sleep! With somebody screaming?" There was a flurry of footsteps and Sue Anne pulled open the door, burst into the hall, blonde hair streaming, eyes wide.

It was Hugh North's turn to blink at a costume—or the lack of one. The G-2 colonel put it down on his list of known facts about this case that Miss Sue Anne Pendleton of Macon, Georgia, slept in the raw. And a well-rounded, melon-breasted, lithe-legged raw it was, too.

Barbara Grafton cried: "*Sue Anne!*" while the men just feasted their eyes. The blonde looked down at herself and clapped a hand to her mouth.

"I forgot," she said and popped back into her room, emerging in a moment wrapped in a fuzzy blue robe and with not a shred of embarrassment visible to the colonel.

"Who screamed?" she demanded. "Why?"

"It probably was a heron or something like that," Barbara

said reassuringly. "Mr. Gregory wants it investigated, though."

"Mebbe I really only wanted to get an eyeful like I just got," North guffawed.

Sue Anne's round blue eyes turned in Hugh's direction and the lush mouth curved. "You're nothing but a Peekin' Pete, I do believe," she giggled. "Aren't you ashamed?"

"Not a bit," the colonel thundered. "Nossir, anything as plumb beautiful as that hadn't oughta be hid."

"Are we investigating screams or not?" Barbara asked icily. "Wesley, knock on Miss Forthier's door."

The millionaire proceeded to the last door in the wing and knocked. The others watched, indifferently at first as though convinced this was a false alarm, and then with quickening concern as the knocks brought no response. Grafton raised his voice.

"Miss Forthier! I say, Miss Forthier, are you all right?"

As the silence stretched, the master of Freebooter's Hall rattled the knob, rapped harder. He turned and looked up at Hugh with eyes that contained fright in their muddy depths. "She's not there," he said in a half whisper. "She doesn't answer."

"She must have taken a pill," Barbara said briskly. "Rap harder. Beat on the door."

"Is it locked?" North asked.

Ward turned the knob, tried the door, looked back at the colonel, nodding. "Locked tight," he said.

"Well, haven't you got a master key?" Terry James asked.

"For goodness' sake, everybody stop sounding so dramatic," Barbara Grafton cried. "The girl's taken a sleeping pill. I remember now, she asked me for one."

"Some pill," Terry James muttered. "Haven't you got a master key somewhere, Wes?"

Grafton seemed dazed. "I don't know," he muttered. "Maybe there's one around somewhere but I don't know where it would be. Besides, she's probably got the door bolted from the inside, too. We'd better try the window."

"Aw, hell, let's bust down the door," Hugh North said. He

shouldered Grafton aside and then drew back, leaning his big body in preparation for a lunge.

"Wait, wait!" Barbara cried. "Don't be ridiculous. Breaking down doors! Here, let me try to wake her up before you do something completely idiotic."

She stepped in front of the colonel and poised her knuckles to rap again when there came a cry from the main hall.

"Mr. Grafton, Mr. Grafton!" Creepy yelled. "Come quick. Dere been an accident in de quarry garden, sar. Miss Forthier —de *other* Miss Forthier—she be stone cold daid, sar!"

[5]

They streamed out of the house, Creepy in the lead, North right behind the Pequot-Bermudian. The boatman carried an electric lantern that painted a wide swath of light across the cochina shell walk and the damp grass. As it swung this way and that in time to Creepy's hurried step, it disturbed and sent leaping into the darkness a half a dozen monster toads such as North had seen earlier.

The first toad brought a shrill screech from Sue Anne Pendleton, a cry that rasped everybody's raw nerves. "What's *that?*" the blonde from Georgia squealed, and leaped into Kenny Trotter's arms, careless of the fuzzy blue robe.

"Oh, for goodness' sake, it's only a toad," Barbara snapped and trotted on, her own dressing gown caught up to her knees, giving her shapely legs free play. "Hundreds of 'em around."

"I'm scared," Sue Anne whimpered. "You'll take care they don't jump on me, won't you, Mr. Trotter?"

"Yes, *may-am*," Kenny promised in an imitative drawl. "You just bet I will."

"Kenny-boy," Hugh bellowed, to remind his aide that things other than armfuls of blondes needed his attention, "where you at?"

The colonel could almost hear Trotter's sigh as the lieutenant released Miss Pendleton and hurried to his boss's side. "Right here, sir," he said. "Sorry, sir."

The pack traversed a formal garden and crunched down a shell walk that headed south, toward Castle Island, then followed a path that wound in and out of a grove of palms, leading away from the shore. They had traveled about a quarter of a mile, North estimated, when Creepy stopped and pointed his lantern downward. The beam of light was swallowed by a pit, dead ahead of him.

Hugh found himself on the fenced edge of a twenty-foot drop, the rim of the quarry from which the coral-and-shell rock had been taken to make Freebooter's Hall. North was to learn later that quarry gardens were common in Bermuda; at the moment he was struck by the immediate thought that this hole was a hell of a convenient thing for a murderer.

Steps chiseled out of the rock led down to the garden below in a wide, gentle sweep. They were not especially steep but they had no railing and were not intended to be negotiated at night without a light, particularly by a woman in loose mules, a stranger to this terrain. A misstep, an off-balance start provoked by one of the toads that littered the place or by a scurrying rat—oh, the murderer had been provided with plenty of reasons for this "accident."

Grafton lurched up beside North, gripping the railing and staring down at the sprawled form of Patricia Forthier below. "Why *her?*" the colonel heard the millionaire murmur.

Barbara Grafton's voice was low, charged with horror. "She tripped on the steps. Poor girl. We've got to get her back to the house and call a doctor for her."

"No use, Mizz Grafton," Creepy said flatly. "She daid. I been down there and looked. Bus' her neck when she fall."

"She *can't* be dead!" Barbara cried, almost petulantly and pushed past the others to descend the curving steps at a reckless pace, considering the menace of her dew-damp gown flapping about her ankles, the uncertain light of Creepy's following lantern.

North came hard on Creepy's heels, Kenny at his elbow, the others following more slowly, feeling their way. When they reached the floor of the quarry, Barbara Grafton hurried to the side of the still form, went down on one knee, and stretched out a hand.

"I beg your pardon, Barby," North said swiftly, "but I wouldn't try movin' her. I had a lotta experience with things like this—the life I been livin' had a lot of accidents in it—and I know if you go movin' her around, you're liable to kill her if she ain't already dead."

Despite his rough words, North's voice had a tinge of command in it sufficient to make Barbara Grafton draw back. Hugh drew her to her feet, turned her toward her husband as Grafton came up. "You let me have a look, Barby," the colonel said, Yahoo's voice gentled. "Ain't no job for a woman."

Patricia Forthier (if that was her real name) lay on her back, one arm flung out at an awkward angle, one leg doubled beneath her. She wore a severe tailored robe over a frill-less nightgown, also tailored, and one foot was still encased in a kid bedroom slipper. Her head was bent in a wry twist that spelled a broken neck. Creepy was right, Colonel North knew immediately; Patricia was dead and had been for some time.

Swiftly, trying not to appear an expert at this, Hugh examined the body while seeming to search for a pulse. Unobtrusively one hand cushioned the girl's head as he raised it from the ground and, unseen, his fingers explored the skull for signs of a blow. There was none.

A trickle of dried blood showed at one corner of the girl's mouth and another dot stained the upper lip under her nostrils. Considering the humid temperature, North estimated that the blood had been spilled at least an hour before.

While the others grouped about him, silent, staring, the G-2 man raised one limp wrist, frowned thoughtfully, and shook his head. Next, he moved aside the wrapper, drew down the nightgown, and placed his big hand under Patricia's full, cold left breast as though hunting for a heartbeat.

Somebody—perhaps Sue Anne—made a muted sound of protest against this exposure and stilled. Hugh's hand stayed in place. The colonel found no heartbeat—he had expected none —but he discovered what he was seeking.

The blood at the mouth and nostrils indicated internal

bleeding and yet the ribs had not been crushed, the torso had not been damaged, even the arms and legs were intact on superficial examination; the snapped neck was the one unlucky break. Hugh was hunting for the wound that had killed Patricia before she had been flung into this pit, and he found it when he had ostensibly sought a heartbeat. Under the left breast, so small that it was hidden by the breast's pendency, was a sliver of a wound.

Slender knife or long needle. And not through the nightgown.

His mouth dragged down, the colonel drew the gown and robe back over Patricia's bosom, climbed to his feet, and brushed at his tight-panted knees. "Ain't no use callin' a doctor," he said. "She's dead, all right."

He turned to Wesley Grafton. "You figger this'll knock our deal in the head?" he asked bluntly.

"No," Grafton muttered. "No, not at all."

"Well, you sure as hell have a funny way of keepin' things private," the colonel boomed. "First, this gal's sister and now her. I reckon the cops will be swarmin' all over the place on account of this. I got half a mind to pack up and get out."

"Well, get out!" It was Sue Anne Pendleton, her pretty face alight with anger as she faced North, the fuzzy blue robe open, her exposed breasts heaving with her indignation. "Just you pack up and get out and see who cares—you and your worry about some old business deal while that poor girl is lyin' there dead!"

Hugh backed away a step. "Well, now," he said, "I was just bein' practical, is all. I didn't mean no disrespect to Miss Forthier, Sue Anne. I apologize all to hell if I said the wrong thing."

Sue Anne spluttered a few incoherencies, then turned and fled to the arms of Barbara Grafton, weeping noisily. Mrs. Grafton murmured quieting nothings. Hugh pushed his sombrero back on his head and rubbed his chin in his discomfort.

"Didn't mean to talk outta turn," he mumbled. "Sorry."

"It's all right," Grafton managed. "We're all upset, naturally." He looked about the dark quarry garden. "I always hated this place," he said thickly. "I would've filled it in if I could but Gail's mother always loved it and—" His voice trailed off.

"That scream you heard must have been Miss Forthier when she went over," Terry James said huskily. "Lost her balance—most likely scared by a toad and—" Like his brother-in-law, he left his sentence unfinished.

Hugh North reached into the breast pocket of his embroidered shirt for a cigarette, extracted one, and snapped his ornate lighter. "I don't know how it happened," he said, his voice echoing off the rock walls about him, "but I know one thing for sure; I hope the cops you've got around here don't think it's too funny that a pair of sisters both got theirs inside a couple of days or so."

He had trouble extinguishing his flaring gas lighter but finally managed to snap out the flame. But not before he had had a good look at the small feathered object that lay half buried in a clump of lantana, close to the steps.

"Now just what in the world is a *wanga* doing here?" he asked himself.

Then his fast-darting mind told him: *Leave it alone and find out.*

[6]

While Grafton was phoning the police at St. George's, Hugh North and Kenny Trotter retired to their apartment.

"What do you know about wangas?" the colonel asked abruptly, the moment the door closed behind them.

Kenny stared. "Is it anything like the samba?"

Hugh's headshake was unsmiling. "No. It's a thing they use in voodoo rites I've seen in Haiti," he said. "A bunch of cock feathers bound around a cork or a block of wood with a needle set in the head."

"So?"

"So there's a wanga lying about twenty feet from Patricia's body," the G-2 man said tersely. "It's hidden, but so poorly that the police are going to spot it right away. And the needle of a wanga is only about two inches long, ordinarily, although this one might be longer—couldn't tell."

"Please, *mon colonel*," the aide begged, "try to put it in one-syllable words so your half-witted assistant can follow."

"Okay, Patricia was killed by a heart wound," North said in a clipped voice. "Stiletto or needle did it. The fall broke her neck, but chances are she was already dead or close to it when she fell."

"And the killer thought he could get away without the stab wound being discovered?" the lieutenant asked disbelievingly.

"Don't know. Grafton's been bragging about his in with this Inspector Boyd—perhaps Boyd would brush off the case as an accident without an autopsy."

"Look, Colonel, a backwoods sheriff would know more than to do anything like that."

"But a backwoods sheriff wouldn't be dealing with a bunch of multimillionaires," North said. "The Grafton family has been here for years—they're mighty important people here-abouts. I'm not saying Boyd will be satisfied without an autopsy; I'm just supposing. And if the killer knew Boyd was likely to be nice and polite to the Graftons—well, you can see the inference."

"But what about this wanga? Could the needle—"

"Too short, I tell you, unless it's an unusual wanga," North said.

"And you didn't put the grab on it?" Kenny asked.

"No. Whoever planted it wanted it to be found as soon as possible, so why play his or her game? We can afford to wait until the police find it—we're not supposed to be that observant, anyway."

"But suppose somebody finds it in the meantime and hides it?" Trotter asked.

"Then we find out who pocketed it and why." North said.

"Creepy can see in the dark. It's funny he didn't spot it, seeing that a thing like that would point a finger at him, the Gombey big shot."

"Creepy did see it," North said grimly. "I watched him and

I saw his eyes slide over to it a dozen times before we left the quarry garden. I wouldn't be surprised but what Creepy planted the wanga in the first place."

"But why, for God's sake?"

"That's what we'll have to find out," North shrugged. "First, though, we've got to decode this pack of cards, and fast. They're expecting me to join them on the veranda and I don't want to keep them waiting."

The colonel went to the attaché case, slipped free the false bottom, and pulled out the playing cards he had taken from Patricia's room. Examination proved that one edge of nearly every card was notched at least once, some in several separated places. Hugh called on his memory to recite the contents of that written page, the paper that quite possibly was the last thing Judy Forthier, Counterintelligence Agent, had written in her life. As he recalled the text, North discarded the padding wordage Judy had needed to fit her key in the "letter."

. . . *died to see* Jack *Quitman . . . taking off* Queen *Elizabeth reviewing the . . . Around* ten *the moon came up and you should have seen Bunny* King *open up like . . .*

Bunny's diamond *was simply . . . a member of the* club *from way back! This time it's a real* heart *case. . . .*

The second paragraph first. Diamond, club, heart; it followed that the spade suit came last. North dealt out the cards in suits, placed the diamonds to the left, then clubs, then hearts and spades.

Jack Quitman, *Queen* Elizabeth, around *ten,* Bunny *King.* Okay, Jack of diamonds, Queen of clubs, ten of hearts, King of spades. Next, sorting in the same relative arrangement, ten of diamonds, Jack of clubs, nine of hearts, Queen of spades. Then nine of diamonds, ten of clubs, eight of hearts, Jack of spades, and so on through the deck.

When the last card joined the pile, Hugh stacked the deck, turned the nicked side of the pack toward him, and brushed graphite from his fingerprint kit into the indentations made by a nail file or manicure scissors on the serrated surface thus provided. This was a method of communication used by secret agents of World War I days; North had heard of its being employed recently only in the direst emergencies; the code was too cumbersome, too weak in the key, to warrant a place in the G-2 man's bag of tricks in this day and age. As he wielded his brush, North told himself that Judy Forthier must have been backed into a real corner to have had to resort to this old-time code.

He finished his brushing, his brow darkening as the graphite filled the indentations. What the hell? He held the pack of cards closer to the light, turned it upside down, held it perpendicular.

Nothing. No lines connected to make a recognizable letter. There was not the faintest resemblance to any known character—Roman, Arabic, or even Chinese!

Swearing softly, North changed the suit sequence in remaking the pack, then scattered the deck to reassemble it in reverse of the instructions contained in the note, going up the ladder of card values instead of down. No good.

Perspiration was bedewing the G-2 colonel's forehead when he finished his last revision and stared at failure. Kenny Trotter made a sympathetic sound but offered no word; experience had taught him that a Hugh North frustrated in what had appeared a simple enough job was about as amenable to flip comment as a bear with a sore tail, and he remained silent until the colonel barked a harsh laugh.

"Man, I've been taken!" Hugh exclaimed. "I thought it was going to be so easy and here I am with my bare face hanging out. Somebody switched cards on me. Or the key."

"You think so?" Kenny asked. "But if somebody knew Judy used the old card-edge code, why didn't that somebody just take the cards, letter and all, instead of planting a phoney deck?"

"Because he or she wanted to see if anybody else was interested in Judy's cards," North explained. "And I may have tipped my hand by taking them out of Patricia's room—if the killer finds out I was the one who got them."

The colonel ran his blunt-fingered hand over his close-cropped hair. "Did Patricia do the switching? Was she really

Judy's sister, after all?" he asked. "It looked as though she was fooling around with these cards—or the real ones—when she was killed; did she know there was such a code or was she just curious about those notches? If she knew about the code, was she a secret agent, a Commie spy, or did she and Judy play with codes when they were kids growing up?"

"Maybe whoever killed Patricia planted the cards and a phoney key just to foul things up," Kenny suggested.

"No, I'm willing to bet the key's okay," North said. "Whoever made the switch didn't know about the key, that's obvious. From the looks of things, Patricia didn't either—the cards were on one table, the letter on another."

He shook his head and grimaced. "A hell of a mess," he admitted.

"What do we do now?" Trotter asked.

"I go down and join the others—or around to the veranda, rather," Hugh North said. "You work on these cards to see if you can get them to make sense. Ten to one you can't but you'll have to give it a try."

Trotter groaned. "Do you know how many possible combinations of fifty-two cards there are?" he asked plaintively.

"I was always lousy at math," Hugh North said heartlessly. "Get goin', podner."

4.

[1]

THE STACCATO roar of a speedboat heralded the approach of the police from Hamilton as dawn blazed in the eastern sky. The group gathered on the screened veranda of Freebooter's Hall left off sipping coffee and eyed the foaming prow of the sleek craft that streaked in toward the coral block pier where Creepy waited.

"That's Boyd," Wesley Grafton said moodily. "I certainly

didn't expect him to be paying us an official visit so soon after the mess about Judy."

"I'm glad it's Inspector Boyd," Gail said. "I like him. He's so nice and British and correct—and stupid."

"Now, now," Grafton objected, "Boyd's not stupid. He's a gentleman—he'll be as easy on us as he can be."

"Easy on us?" Barbara's eyebrows were half-mooned. "You sound as though we were ripe for grilling. It was an accident, pure and simple, wasn't it? Awkward, of course, coming so soon after Judy's drowning, but no more than foul coincidence, after all."

"Of course," Grafton muttered and rose from his chair. "Better go down and meet them." He left the veranda and started down the cochina shell walk.

Barbara James Grafton watched her husband make his way toward the pier. "Poor Wes," she said. "By the way he's acting, a person would think he's responsible for both these terrible things." She sipped her coffee before she added deliberately: "Which he is, of course, in a way."

"What a perfectly rotten thing to say," Gail Grafton cried.

Barbara cast a cool glance at her stepdaughter. "Purely theoretical, dear Gail," she explained. "If Wes hadn't hired Judy as his secretary she wouldn't have been here to go swimming and drown and so, of course, her sister wouldn't have come to Freebooter's Hall at all. For heaven's sake, I'm not suggesting your father murdered those women."

"And you're forgetting, dear Barbara," Gail returned, as coolly, "that it was you who hired Judy Forthier as *your* secretary. For reasons best known to yourself."

The two beautiful women exchanged glances in which Hugh North could almost hear the clash of steel. Still, Barbara's voice was quiet, faintly amused, when she said: "Wrong again, Gail. I don't know what your father has told you, but he was the one who chose Miss Forthier for my secretary— and appropriated her for his own when Wilson, his secretary, got so conveniently ill."

"That's not so!" Gail replied indignantly. "I happen to know—"

"Oh, for goodness' sake, let's not have any fussin' this morning," Sue Anne Pendleton wailed. "We all ought to be so sad about poor Miss Patricia that nothing else matters."

"She's right," said bulky Terry James. "You two females can quit sniping at each other for a few minutes at least, can't you? You're giving Yahoo the wrong impression. He'll begin to think this isn't one great big happy family if you keep this up."

"Don't mind me," North grunted. "I'm used to family arguments—the Gregorys were always raisin' hell with each other when I was growin' up. I remember the time Ma fetched the old man alongside the head with a hot fryin' pan. All us kids wore fatback grease burns for weeks."

"Well, think of the gendarmes then, Barby," James said. "You wouldn't want Inspector Boyd to get any wrong ideas about the loving-kindness that rules here, would you?"

Gail Grafton shot her playboy stepuncle a venomous glance. "Perhaps the gendarmes would like to know what you were doing rapping on Patricia's door at two o'clock in the morning," she snapped.

Sue Anne's bright red lips made an "O" as she sat up in her chair with a start. "Was that you?" she asked Terry.

James made an attempt to laugh, but it did not quite succeed. "I was just trying to be sociable, that's all," he said. "I felt like a moonlight swim and I was trying to get somebody to go with me."

"Patricia Forthier?" Townley Ward asked unbelievingly.

"Well, I got a little mixed up with my rooms," Terry explained. "I thought I was tapping gently at Sue Anne's chamber door, not Miss Forthier's. Nobody answered, anyway, either Patricia or Sue Anne." He squinted at the blonde from Macon. "And where were *you?*" he demanded.

"Oh, I was right there all the time," the blonde replied, her chin rising. "I heard you bangin' next door and then you started in on my door, and I looked at my clock and I knew whoever it was must be awful tight so I stayed put until you stopped bangin' and went away."

"I was *not* banging," Terry said severely. "I was tapping, I tell you. You ought to know the difference between—ah, here's Bermuda's Sherlock Holmes, Inspector Boyd himself, with his Dr. Watson, Constable Lunt."

Hugh measured this British police inspector as he came up the steps with Wesley Grafton. Boyd was a stocky, mustached man in sun helmet, white linen suit, white buck shoes, and a slightly vacant expression. He was trailed by an alert-looking young constable, neat in the gray and silver uniform of the Bermuda police force.

"You know everybody here except Mr. Gregory and Miss Pendleton, I believe," Wesley Grafton said. "Inspector Boyd, Miss Pendleton, Mr. Gregory."

"Hi," said Sue Anne.

"Call me Yahoo," North said and rose to shake hands.

The inspector's pale blue eyes were mildly incredulous as he viewed the raiment of Yahoo Gregory. "How d'ja do?" he asked in a tired voice. "Believe you have a sec't'ry somewhere about, eh?"

North's surprise came close to breaking through his front. Why had Grafton found it necessary to brief Boyd about Kenny in that short walk from the pier to the house? "Yeah, he's in the room," the G-2 colonel nodded. "You want him?"

"Understand he heard Miss Forthier scream," Boyd explained wearily. To Grafton he said: "Appreciate it if you'd have somebody ask Mr.—Trotter, is it?—to join us, please."

Grafton rang for one of the maids and sent her to Kenny's room with the "invitation."

"Constable," Boyd sighed to the young man in the silver and gray uniform, "you'd better go down to the quarry garden. Take the stretcher with you. Have Creepy show you the way. Look around like a good chap, will you?"

Lunt saluted and left to join Creepy, who had stationed himself at the foot of the steps. Inspector Boyd accepted a cup of coffee, deposited his topee on a wicker table, and dropped into a chair with another sigh.

"You people seem to be accident prone, what?" he asked plaintively. "First a drowning and now this. Can you tell me what happened, exactly?"

Wesley Grafton hunched his thick shoulders. "Pretty obvious, as you'll see. Girl missed her footing on those damned steps and took a fall, broke her neck."

"Pity." Boyd sipped his coffee. "Why was she out there, d'you know?"

"I think I can answer that," Barbara Grafton offered. "She was terribly upset about her sister, of course, and she had trouble sleeping. She asked me if I had any sedatives and I told her no, although I do have some sleeping pills—my doctor in Hamilton warned me against passing them around, you see." The statuesque brunette shook her head. "I told her I didn't have any, but now I wish I'd taken the chance and given her one."

"You think she was out strolling, then, to tire herself enough to sleep?" Boyd asked.

"What else is there to think?" Barbara parried.

The inspector sipped again and dragged his eyes around to North. "Now, Mr. Gregory, mind telling us about that scream?"

Hugh frowned thoughtfully, thumbing his jaw. "I been thinkin' about that, podner," he said slowly. "Seems to me my secretary and me thought it came from the east wing, the part of the house furtherest away from our rooms. But that quarry garden ain't over there—it's almost due south of our rooms."

There was a stark silence and then North lifted his fringe-shirted shoulders in a shrug. "Hard to judge noises, though," he added. "Specially in a strange place with the wind blowin'."

"Mr. Grafton tells me you examined the body," Boyd said with supreme disinterest.

"Sure," Hugh answered promptly. "I didn't want anybody liftin' her in case she was still alive and had a broken back or somethin'. Sure, I looked at her. She was dead, all right. Busted neck. Maybe you'll find some other things when you have your whaddaya call it—autopsy—but she had a busted neck, for sure."

Boyd nodded indifferently, returned to Barbara Grafton.

"You said Miss Forthier asked you for a sleeping pill—you two were rather chummy, eh?"

Barbara's headshake was emphatic. "Heavens, no! I wasn't at all what anybody could call friendly with her. She was a— difficult person to be friendly with. Perhaps that was understandable in the situation but she—well, frankly, I found her rather a bore. I think she and Gail struck up some kind of friendship but—"

"I?" Gail's tone was stunned by surprise. "Why, Barbara, I don't think I spoke half a dozen words to her!"

The inspector moved his weary eyes to Wesley Grafton. "I understand this woman called you from New York when Miss Judy Forthier disappeared. At that time did she offer any proof that she was Miss Forthier's sister? Or did she later, when you met her in Hamilton?"

"Why—why, no," Grafton acknowledged. "No, I didn't ask for any identification. I didn't think it was necessary. Why?"

The inspector's knuckle came up to brush the mustache. "Rather odd thing's happened," he said. "Matter of fact, I'd have come over here today even if this thing hadn't brought me here. Y'see, the C.I.D. chaps who make it their business to interest themselves in such things sent word to my chief in Hamilton late last night that their inquiries show Miss Judy Forthier had no living relatives closer than a second cousin who lives in Florida. As far as they could find out, Judy Forthier was an only child with no sisters at all."

The inspector looked around the group, his pale blue eyes very bland.

"Peculiar, what?" he asked.

[2]

Which, Colonel Hugh North told himself, as the people on the veranda broke into startled voice, *settles that; our Patricia was a phoney.*

This, of course, raised the other natural questions in the colonel's mind: Was Patricia a spy for other business interests, was she a foreign agent, or was she a chiseler scheming to steal a slice of anything valuable left by Judy Forthier? Whatever game Patricia had been playing, the G-2 man grimaced inwardly, she had found out too late that it was played for keeps in this league.

Wesley Grafton was the first to find coherent voice. "You mean she was an impostor?" he cried. "But—but why in the world would she want to come in here like that?"

Boyd shrugged languidly. "I'd say that's what we should try to find out," he replied with no enthusiasm. "It's been suggested that this woman may have seen a possibility of threatening a suit for damages, accepting a quick settlement, and making off. Only a guess, of course, but it sounds as reasonable as anything else right now."

"She never mentioned a lawsuit," Grafton growled. "Matter of fact, she kept insisting that her sister—well, Judy—couldn't have drowned because she was such a good swimmer."

"It could be that she was laying the groundwork for a negligence claim against you," Inspector Boyd offered. "She might even have had an idea about criminal action charges—claim your beach wasn't sufficiently protected and all that sort of thing."

"Ridiculous," Barbara Grafton snorted disdainfully. "The girl was not the kind who'd dare start any trouble—she was positively afraid of her own shadow."

Boyd flickered a glance in Barbara's direction. "Afraid?" he asked softly. "You mean she feared for her own life; is that it?"

Barbara's reply was as cool as the eyes which met the inspector's. "Of course I didn't mean that and you know it," she said. "What I meant was that she was always apologizing for being underfoot, making us all uncomfortable with her everlasting whining."

"Oh, Barbara!" Gail Grafton exclaimed. "You shouldn't speak of her that way."

"Well, she was," the beautiful brunette said. "I don't know what that woman was up to, but I'd bet anything she didn't have in mind anything that would require as much courage as a shakedown or blackmail."

"Blackmail!" Wesley Grafton exploded. "What in God's name would she have to blackmail us about?"

The hostess of Freebooter's Hall swung her lovely head about to stare at her husband. "Nothing, of course," she said, too sweetly. "I'm sure that all our pasts are spotless. Not one of us has ever done anything we'd pay to keep off the front page."

"Speak for yourself, Barby," Terry James said with a strained laugh.

Hugh considered his next step for a moment; then decided to make the move and observe reactions. "Funny thing," he said in Yahoo's clamorous voice. "That gal, whatever her name really was, walked up here from the dock with me last night —early this mornin'. Had somethin' on her mind, all right. Just before Wes, here, come along she said somethin' about—well, this is the way I heard it—somethin' about thinkin' her sister, the real Miss Forthier, was maybe murdered."

"*Murdered!*" It was a joined cry from Grafton, Gail, Barbara, Sue Anne Pendleton, and Townley Ward.

"Uh-huh," the colonel nodded. "I—well, I thought maybe she was stoned, to tell you the truth. But that's what she said."

Gail Grafton eyed the bogus uranium king with an icy stare. "You're sure you're not indulging in some prairie humor?" she said.

"Now just a moment, Gail," Grafton protested as North drew himself up in hurt surprise. "That's no way to talk to Mr. Gregory."

"Sorry," Gail said briefly, "but, frankly, I just don't believe it."

"I'm with you, Gail," Terry James said. "Maybe Yahoo misunderstood what the woman said." He eyed the colonel with a level stare. "You had a couple of drinks last night yourself, didn't you?"

"Maybe a thimbleful," North acknowledged. "Aw, forget it if it gets you folks all het up. I just thought the inspector, here, oughta know." *And not a one of them showed any vio-*

lent reaction except the natural shock to be expected when I mentioned murder. We've got a clever actor here. Or actress.

The touchy situation was eased by Kenny Trotter's appearance. Inspector Boyd managed to summon the energy to get out of his chair and extend a limp hand. "Name's Boyd," he sighed. "You're Mr. Gregory's sec't'ry, eh?" As Kenny nodded, the man in the white linen suit asked: "Now where was it that the scream came from?"

Trotter did not look at his colonel; he did not have to. As he had entered the veranda he had shot a glance at Hugh and had gotten the signal—*Play it according to the original script* —in a way that nobody not trained in G-2 means of silent communication could have possibly intercepted.

"Why, from the east wing, sir," Trotter said. "Didn't Mr. Gregory tell you?"

"Ah, yes, he did, come to think of it," Boyd nodded. "And what time did you say that was?"

Trotter appeared to be casting back. "Oh, about three-thirty, quarter to four," he answered and then corrected himself. "No, Miss Grafton said it was quarter to four when we woke her so it must have been earlier—say, three-twenty-five."

"Don't go by my watch," Gail Grafton said. "It runs slow most of the time—the salt air or something."

"And Creepy says he found the body at about the same time," Inspector Boyd said. "Creepy told us he was out shooting rats and went down to the quarry garden to see if there were any to be had there."

"Yeah, he was shootin' rats, all right," North agreed. "Kenny and me can vouch for that. Got us outta bed, bangin' around. We went out to see what was goin' on."

"For heaven's sake," Barbara Grafton put in, "what do we have here, a murder investigation? Everybody checking time and verifying things. It was an accident, I tell you! I don't know why Patricia came here or what she was up to, but it was still an accident."

"Sure," Colonel North said. "You look over the body and where it happened and you'll see, Inspector."

"Well, perhaps I ought," Boyd said reluctantly. "Wouldn't

bother but—well, you must admit this case has its curious side, the pseudo sister, the woman going walking at that time of night after telling Mr. Gregory she thought Judy Forthier had been murdered—"

"You don't believe that, do you, Boyd?" It was Townley Ward who interjected the question.

"Believe what, that Judy Forthier was murdered?" the man from Hamilton asked. "Oh dear, I hope not—I've already reported that to be an accidental drowning, y'know. But perhaps, I'll have to revise my report before the investigation's finished, what?"

"Investigation?" Grafton cried. "You mean you're going to make a big case out of this? You can't do that—we've got an important conference coming up today. Sir George Pakenham is due to arrive here this morning and—and Mr. Gregory is anxious to get back to the States and—and—"

"Oh, do go on with your conference," Inspector Boyd said apologetically. "I shall try to keep out of your way, I promise. Now, let's go down and see what's what in the garden, shall we?" To Barbara he said: "It won't be necessary for you ladies to come; just the gentlemen."

"Damned inconvenient," Grafton muttered. "Haven't had a full night's sleep and here we have to—"

"Oh, pipe down, Wes," Townley Ward interrupted. "Of course we want to cooperate with the inspector."

"Hell, yes," North said, heaving himself out of his chair. "If there's one thing I want to do it's stay on the right side of the law. With this phoney Forthier sister here, I want all the investigation I can get—I want to be damned sure this deal of yours is as safe as you claim it is, Grafton."

"That's right, Yahoo," Gail Grafton said bitterly. "With a dead woman in the quarry garden, another drowned, with the police mumbling something about murder, you just keep on worrying about whether your deal is safe. That's the important thing, isn't it?"

"That'll be enough, Gail," Wesley Grafton barked. "Instead of being unpleasant to our guest, you might go over to Hidden Bay and tell young Gibbons that if he doesn't get his boat out of there at once I'll come over there and make trouble for him, personally."

"Stan Gibbons?" Inspector Boyd murmured. "Is he on Plunder Island, too?"

"He spent the night aboard his boat in the bay," Gail said defiantly. "And don't worry, Father, he won't trespass on your own private ocean any more."

"Well, suppose we let him trespass a bit longer," Boyd said smoothly. "Tell Mr. Gibbons I'd appreciate it very much if he'd join us here at Freebooter's Hall."

"Why?" Gail demanded. "Why drag Stan into this?"

Inspector Boyd's smile was as untroubled as a child's. "No special reason, my dear," he said quietly, "but in this peculiar case with its peculiar sidelights I'd rather Stan Gibbons and everybody else who was on or near Plunder Island last night stay around to answer a few questions."

He turned away from Gail Grafton's hot eyes and said: "Shall we join the constable, gentlemen?"

[3]

The body of "Patricia Forthier" was covered by a tarpaulin when the little group reached the quarry garden. Constable Lunt was examining the ground at the far end of the pit, and Creepy sat on a bench not far from the base of the stone steps.

It was a place of beauty in the just-risen sun. The garden blazed with hibiscus, euphorbia, lantana, plumbago, a dozen varieties of jasmine, oleander, allamanda, and other plants which North could not identify. Their perfume hung heavy in the early morning dampness, and birds sounded an incongruously gay litany in their salute to the day. The scene was one in which sudden death, death by murder, should have had no part; and yet that mute, still form under the canvas would not be dispelled from any mind present, no matter how perfumed the morning breeze, how sweet the birds' welcome to the morning.

Inspector Boyd looked about him. "Nasty things, quarry

gardens," he observed mildly. "Ought to be a law against 'em. Pardon me a mo' while I check with my man."

Constable Lunt and the man in the white suit withdrew a distance from the group beside the body—Grafton, Ward, James, Trotter, and North. The two policemen put their heads together, and the G-2 colonel could see Lunt explaining earnestly while Boyd permitted himself an occasional nod. As they talked, the constable fumbled in a pocket of his tunic and finally passed over to Boyd the small tuft of feathers which North had seen earlier, half-hidden in the foliage, the wanga.

The colonel shot a look at Creepy on his bench. The Pequot-Bermudian sat with hunched shoulders, staring at the ground, his whole attitude suggesting nothing more than final resignation. *They've found your wanga and your job's done, eh?*

For the wanga certainly pointed a finger of suspicion at Creepy. Yet the boatman had let it lie there although he must have seen it if, indeed, he had not planted it himself. Why? And if Creepy actually had used the feathered thing, why had he, instead of letting a ricocheted .22 slug be blamed—Creepy had set the stage carefully enough for that.

Hugh turned back to see Inspector Boyd coming toward the group about the body, drawing a cigarette from his pocket, lighting it. The man in the white suit looked down at the tarpaulin and hesitated, almost as though he already knew what he would find and deplored the necessity of uncovering murder and the task it would set for him.

"Well, let's get at it," he said finally and knelt beside the dead woman who had claimed to be Judy Forthier's sister. Uncovered, the woman's face was a ghastly gray with dull, staring eyes, gaping mouth, and slack chin. The blood at her mouth and nostrils was black now and the skin had assumed that sickening tough-spongy texture which dead bodies, particularly those of persons who die violently, so often take on.

Boyd was professionally moving the neck, testing the corpse's rigidity. He did not dislodge the robe or nightgown to search for the breast wound North had found; the G-2 colonel surmised that Lunt had already found that wound or that Boyd was perfectly willing to let a thorough examination wait on the post-mortem doctor. The inspector's cursory examination concluded, he rose to his feet.

"Afraid you're right, Mr. Gregory," he said with characteristic ennui. "A broken neck and Lord knows what else." He glanced up at the steps above them. "Must have fallen at least fifteen feet—enough to snap anybody's neck, I'd say." He covered the body again with the tarpaulin, dragged at his cigarette. "Pardon me again. Must speak to Lunt." He walked away.

There was a silence among the men until Townley Ward said: "Too bad you had to bring up that business about what Patricia said about Judy being murdered. If you hadn't, Boyd would probably write this off as a simple accident. Now, I don't know."

"Well, I'm sorry if I talked outta turn," Hugh replied, "but I reckon Boyd would have had to poke into this anyway, wouldn't he, seein' as how this gal was a phoney?"

Townley nodded reluctantly. "I suppose you're right. Dammit, Wes, couldn't you have been a little more careful about checking up on this woman? Or did you perhaps arrange her coming here?"

Grafton's bloodshot eyes were angry. "That's a hell of a thing to say," he retorted. "How do I know she wasn't somebody you planted here to do your dirty work?"

"Hold it," Terry James said warningly. "Let's not start fighting among ourselves—not now. This woman could have been working for any one of a dozen people, Townley. How do we know she wasn't from Paratina?"

Hugh's face did not move a muscle; neither did Kenny's. Both men repressed the upsurge of excitement within them; they had the State Department's answer to one big question and it had been handed them on a silver platter by Terry James.

Grafton and Ward both shot a black look at the husky playboy who, for reasons that North could not understand now, had been included in this secret deal. "Keep your voice down, you fool!" Grafton hissed. "This place echoes—don't spill everything you know to Boyd."

"Sorry," Terry said, "but my question stands."

"As far as that goes," Hugh broke in heartily, "you fellers don't know for sure I didn't send her on ahead to find out how the land lay, do you?" He held up a big hand as Ward and Grafton began their protests. "Oh, I don't mind," he went on. "I've gotten used to partners in a deal doin' everything they can to make sure the others ain't givin' them a reamin'. But if you want me to say it, I never set eyes on her in my life 'til I met her last night. Not that I expect you to take my word for it."

"Don't worry," Townley Ward said with a brief laugh, "we'd have known it if you'd sent an advance agent. We're not entirely stupid, Yahoo."

"How about the dook, Pakenham?" the colonel asked. "You think he'd want to have somebody here protectin' his interests until he got here, maybe?"

Both Ward and Townley shook their heads. It was Terry James who voiced the probability that was high in North's mind. "You guys are forgetting one thing," the playboy said. "If somebody wanted Patricia here, the same person gave her an excuse to move in. That means Judy may have been gotten out of the way so Patricia could come here, doesn't it?"

Wesley Grafton brushed a hand over his sagging, pouchy-eyed face. "I refuse to believe it," he said. "No, Judy drowned and this woman saw a chance to get some money out of me somehow, and—"

"Meaning you were doing something else besides dictating letters to little Judy when you were in your office with the door locked?" Terry jeered.

"*Hold it!*" Townley Ward barked, but not in time. Wesley Grafton uttered a strangled curse and swung on his big-shouldered brother-in-law with a roundhouse right that a child could have avoided, but which Terry James ducked into. The millionaire's fist caught James spang on the chin, there was a satisfying crack, and Barbara's brother went staggering back, caught his heel in a trailing vine, and landed on the ground with a thump beside "Patricia Forthier's" body.

James scrambled to his feet and lunged at Grafton but the gaudy figure of "Yahoo Gregory" blocked the way. "Simmer down, son," North counseled. "You already caused enough stink for one mornin'. Now that inspector is really gonna have some questions to ask."

"God damn you," James panted, glaring at Grafton past Hugh's shoulder. "I hope Boyd asks you where you were when Judy disappeared. I hope he asks you about the clothes you planted on the—"

"*Shut up!*" Townley Ward blared.

"No, no," Inspector Boyd said wearily from behind Grafton. "Let Mr. James speak out, if y'don't mind. Interestin'."

Hugh released Terry and turned toward the inspector. "Just a little family squabble, Cap'n," he grinned. "You know how it is with brother-in-laws—or mebbe you ain't got such an animal."

"Oh, indeed I have," Boyd said pleasantly, "and they're both splendid chaps. And what were you saying, Mr. James, about the planted clothes?"

"Nothing," Terry muttered sullenly, a hand to his bruised jaw.

"No? Well, p'raps we can talk that over later, eh?" Boyd drawled. "Meanwhile, I've got something to say. Quite astounding, actually. Constable Lunt's found some things that indicate this woman's fall was no simple accident at all. She was *made* to fall and I'm afraid that's awkward, gentlemen. That could be murder."

His tired drawl did not quicken but there was the suggestion of a bite beneath its weary flow. "Terribly sorry, but I must warn you all—the way things are done, y'know—that you mustn't try to leave Plunder Island 'til I say you can. To put it bluntly, I rather fear you've got a killer amongst you."

"Listen—" Wesley Grafton began in a choked voice but he got no further.

"Ain't no use botherin' de gentlemen no more, Inspector. I

was de one that made de lady fall. You know that—de constable found de wanga."

And as they all turned, Creepy, the skipper of *Amphitrite*, stretched forth his hands as though to let them be linked by a pair of handcuffs.

[4]

"Poor Creepy," Hugh said later to Kenny Trotter in their quarters in Freebooter's Hall. "All those heroics and they'll stand up just as long as it takes the post-mortem doctor in Hamilton to find that breast wound."

"I don't get it," Kenny admitted. "What's Creepy's angle, taking the blame for this murder?"

The G-2 colonel finished his inspection of the rooms (one required to make sure the doctored bug had not been replaced during their absence) and moved toward the telephone on the desk in a corner of the sitting room. "Creepy is being a knight in shining armor," he said. "I'll tell you all about it after I let headquarters know about Paratina."

The colonel put through his call to the actual headquarters of the Yahoo Gregory uranium interests in Salt Lake City, Utah. There, he spoke with one "George L. Van Huse," who could be readily identified by any interested listener-in as the general manager of the Gregory enterprises and Yahoo's second in command. Since G-2 had moved into this case, one of North's brother agents had occupied Van Huse's desk, waiting for just such a phone call.

Yahoo spoke lengthily and profanely about various matters, all of which might have been vitally important to those persons connected with uranium production, the New York stock market, or possibly to a collector of off-color jokes, but which mentioned not one word about the murder of a woman posing as Judy Forthier's sister or even hinted at the name of the Central American banana republic in which Washington was so vitally interested, Paratina.

When Terry James had blurted the name Paratina as "Patricia Forthier's" possible place of origin, Hugh North's memory had cast up all pertinent facts about that little republic. It presently was struggling to keep alive a truly democratic form of government after years under benign and not so benign dictatorships. The recent elections had been marred by Red-triggered riots, which had nearly toppled the democratic political structure headed by President Ramón Quedado, and Washington had held its breath until the Quedado regime had succeeded in stamping out the strikes, sabotage, and terror led by Moscow-financed hoodlums.

So now that Paratina had finally managed to embark on a shaky program of economic and political recovery, Wesley Grafton, Townley Ward, Sir George Pakenham, and "Yahoo Gregory" intended to start havoc so they could make a lot of money, eh? Not if Hugh North could help it—and with this word to G-2 and through G-2 to the State Department, it seemed that he *could* help it, immensely.

The code he used in his rambling conversation with "Van Huse" was intricate and unbreakable, set up only for this one case. When he had finished gabbing, Hugh had told G-2 that Paratina was the hot spot threatened by this combine of millionaires and that he would have more definite information after Sir George Pakenham arrived and the syndicate got down to cases; meanwhile, Counterintelligence agents in the little Central American republic were to be alerted to the fact that trouble was being brewed in Bermuda, thousands of miles away.

He hung up, finally, and took time out to light a cigarette, mix himself a mild Scotch and soda (a respite before plunging back into bourbon and branchwater), and dropped into an easy chair.

"About Creepy," he said, "I wouldn't be surprised if Boyd had to bring him back here from Hamilton as soon as the autopsy's finished, if he doesn't hold him as a material witness or something. Doubt they do that, though; the British are much more rigid about such things than we are—book 'em or turn 'em loose is their motto."

"You think Creepy planted the wanga?"

North nodded. "Pretty sure. For some reason he wanted to be accused of Patricia's death."

"Well, maybe he did stab her with the wanga needle and got remorseful," Trotter offered.

Hugh shook his head. "No, I don't think Creepy even knows about the stab wound any more than Boyd or Lunt do. That wound never was made by the wanga needle—too deep."

"Just what is a wanga, *mon colonel?*"

"I told you; it's a few feathers fastened with waxed cord to a cork or a little block of wood, with a needle set in the head," North explained. "I've seen several of them in Haiti."

"But Creepy's no Haitian."

"Oh, I don't doubt they're fairly common all over this part of the world—I just saw mine in Haiti. The wanga started out as a blowgun dart and may still be used in some of the hill countries of the Caribbean, for all I know, but somewhere along the line the wanga got to be part of the voodoo ceremony. I believe the sacrificial animals and fowl had to be killed with a sacred wanga originally—anyway, it's a big thing in the voodoo rites."

"And Creepy's supposed· to be a what-do-you-call-it—the Bermuda brand of voodoo."

"Gombey," North supplied. "Creepy's a priest of the Gombeys."

"Well, why the whole weird business—what was Creepy telling Boyd when you got within earshot so neatly before our languid inspector caught wise and shooed us all back to the house?"

"Creepy said he threw the wanga at Patricia while she was at the head of the steps; the thing brushed her face and frightened her into a fall.·Remember, Creepy is known to be able to see in the dark—he gets his rats that way—and he *could* possibly have brushed Patricia's face with the wanga, if he had thrown the thing. Suppose she was already jittery over the toads; wouldn't she about jump out of her skin when she felt those feathers?"

"Oh, come now," Kenny protested, "who's going to swallow

that? Is she supposed to have fallen and conveniently broken her neck?"

"That's Creepy's story, not mine," North said. "It won't stand up, of course. The autopsy will show that Creepy's a valiant liar who planted the wanga to take the blame."

"Off who—or whom, whichever it is?"

"I'd say Gail Grafton," Hugh North explained calmly.

"Gail Grafton!"

"Sure, you told me yourself that Creepy's madly in love with Gail, in the most noble sense of the word."

"But—but—"

"It's only a guess, of course, but I think our rat-hunting friend saw Gail abroad last night when she was supposed to be in bed. I got that idea the minute she consulted her wrist watch at the bedroom door, complaining about the noise. What woman wears a wrist watch to bed, even a diamond wrist watch? Gail wasn't roused from any slumber when we called."

· "You think Gail did Patricia in?"

North shook his head. "Can't imagine a motive," he said. "No, my guess is that she was on Stan Gibbons' boat, studying ichthyology or something. Creepy saw her hurrying home before cock's crow, and when he found Patricia dead he was afraid Gail would have some pretty tall explaining to do. Rather than have his goddess suspected of heaving Patricia over the cliff, Creepy planted the wanga to incriminate himself, then gave himself up to keep Boyd from going any further with his questions."

"Which proves Creepy didn't kill Patricia," Kenny Trotter said. "Scratch one suspect."

"Not so fast. Suppose Creepy did kill Patricia with the knife or needle or whatever was used? What better way to clear himself than the wanga bit, knowing it wouldn't stand a chance of sending him to the gallows? Oh, Creepy, he's the noble one, everybody would say, but how silly of him! These simple-minded natives! And Creepy would go around tipping his cap to all the brilliant white folks while enjoying a laugh."

"You think he—"

"No, I don't. Not yet. I haven't a single thing to connect Judy or Patricia with Creepy. Or with Grafton or Ward or James or Barbara or Gail or Sue Anne."

"Sue Anne! Now, you're not going to tell me that that delicious bit òf the Old South could be mixed up in a murder!"

North looked pained. "When are you going to learn that a girl's looks, build, and sex appeal have nothing whatever to do with her ability to commit murder?"

"Never," Kenny admitted promptly. "Or at least not 'til I'm seventy." He considered that statement for a moment and then amended it. "Make it eighty," he said.

North resumed his drink. Kenny dragged on his cigarette and then crushed it out. "What about Terry's crack about the clothes, before Townley Ward shut him up?"

"Guessing again," North replied, "I'd say Grafton planted some of Judy's clothes on the beach near the Pass to hide Judy's suicide—which requires taking it for granted that Grafton believes the suicide note."

"Why do you suppose Grafton told you about the suicide in the first place?" the young lieutenant asked.

"Grafton needs Yahoo Gregory's dough desperately—he's scared to death Yahoo will pull out of the deal," Hugh explained. "He took a calculated risk in telling me about the suicide, but he wanted to prove he was leveling with me. And remember, he'd been drinking. Maybe he regrets it now, but it was his impulse at that moment to make a friend in this deal by sharing that confidence."

"Make a friend? You don't think Ward and Pakenham are really his buddy-buddies?" Kenny asked.

"Don't know. But if Patricia was working for one of the partners and wasn't just a chiseler on her own, her boss wanted the Paratina deal to fall through or something like that. Otherwise, why would Patricia tell me about her suspicions of Judy's murder? She couldn't have been a Red agent —the Commies want the Paratina thing to succeed, and Patricia would never have risked scaring Yahoo off if she was paid by Moscow."

"There's this angle, though," Trotter said. "Suppose the

Reds just want Yahoo Gregory scared out so they can put their own man, more closely tied to them, into the syndicate. Then Patricia could have been a Commie agent."

"I won't buy that," Hugh North argued. "Grafton set up this deal and he thought he was mighty careful picking his partners. The Reds couldn't just move a stooge in; Grafton wouldn't stand still for it."

"Maybe our Wesley's so hard up he'd have to take anything he could find to sub for Yahoo," Kenny persisted. "Either that or be out in the cold."

"There's something in that, I agree," Hugh nodded. "But we could make guesses like this all day and we've got work to do. You'd better get back at those cards. Where are they?"

The lieutenant looked over at the desk North had recently quit. "They're taped to the underside of a drawer," he said gloomily. "I haven't gotten anywhere with them. I don't think there's any message on them, if you want my opinion."

"Keep trying," Hugh said cheerily. "If you think you've got it rough, think of me drinking that damned bourbon and whooping around as Yahoo Gregory. I'll switch jobs with you any time."

There was a tap on the door. North was out of his chair, his voice booming. "Come in, come in!" he cried. "We're decent."

It was the same pretty housemaid on whom North had pressed the ten-dollar bill a few hours earlier. She bobbed a curtsey but she did not show her teeth in the usual smile. "Mr. Grafton asks can you join him in de office, sar," she said glumly. "Told me to tell you Sar George Pakenham done arrive. I show you de way, if you like."

"I like," North said enthusiastically.

The girl hesitated and then blurted: "Mr. Gregory, what they do with Creepy, sar?"

"I don't think they'll keep him long," the G-2 colonel said reassuringly.

"Dey oughtn't," the maid said with a shake of her head. "Creepy, he wouldn't do a thing like dat. He—he's just tryin' to keep 'em from findin' out about—"

And before North could stop her, the girl whirled and ran down the hall.

Sir George Pakenham turned out to be the antithesis of the stage Englishman. Instead of being a cadaverous individual in drooping mustache, monocle, and deerstalker hat, he proved to be a towering, baldheaded man with horn-rimmed glasses, a deep tan, and the mouth of a mako shark. The handshake he gave Hugh North, though, was as limp as the fictional Lord Cholmsley-Olmsley's might have been.

"How do you do," he said coldly when North was introduced and immediately turned his back on the colonel to speak to Ward.

"I'm fine, thanks," North said, breaking through Pakenham's words to Townley. "How's it goin' with you?"

The Englishman turned back slowly, gave North a look that was an insult, and then presented his broad back a second time. "Let's get on with it, Ward," he said curtly. "I'd like to make this as brief as possible. Got a trip to Kenya scheduled for the first, and there's God's own number of things to be taken care of here and there before then."

"Dunno as the police will let you leave here now you're here," North cried, undaunted by the two snubs. "Didn't Wes tell you about this place bein' quarantined?"

Pakenham granted Hugh a thin, unpleasant smile. "To set your mind at ease, I've already been assured by Inspector Boyd that I can leave when I'm ready," he said.

"Well, hell, that ain't fair," North protested. "You mean us Amurricans gotta stay here while—"

"It's just that Sir George wasn't on the island when—when it happened," Grafton broke in. "He could hardly be connected with the case, could he?"

"Why couldn't he have sent that woman here, like I said?" Hugh asked.

"Sir George?" Grafton asked. He seemed shocked by the suggestion. Pakenham himself merely uttered a suppressed snort.

"Why not?" North pursued ruthlessly. "Hell, he's as anxious

as I am to look out for his own herd, dook or no dook. I don't know what kind of stake he's got in thisyere game—hell, I don't even know the name of the game, yet, remember—but I guess George, here, likes a buck as well as the next feller."

Townley Ward's voice was charged with anxiety and North could imagine the younger multimillionaire seeing Sir George Pakenham saying to hell with dealing with this oaf, packing his papers, and flying away. "Let's get down to business," Ward said. "Yahoo, you're right when you say it's time you learned the name of the game, as you put it. Wes, do you want to explain the set-up or would you rather Sir George did?"

"I set it up; I'll lay it out," Grafton said gruffly. "Before we start in, though, who wants a drink?"

Yahoo had to have his bourbon but the other two said no. Sir George, visibly irritated at the start both by Yahoo's crudities and Grafton's thirst, drummed his fingers on the conference table until Grafton finally took his place and began his explanation of the Big Deal.

It was about as Hugh North had expected. An ambitious colonel in the Paratina army, one Guerra, was ready to let loose a revolt in return for sizable contributions "to be spent for arms and to enlist the services of other true patriots." If and when the revolution succeeded, the syndicate would be guaranteed mining and oil monopolies which, according to Grafton, would return satisfactory dividends on the "investment."

"Sounds okay," North said when Grafton had finished, "but how do we know this Guerra won't just tell us all to kiss his foot when he gets in the driver's seat? What guarantees we got besides his word?"

Townley Ward put it bluntly: "Guerra knows he wouldn't live twenty-four hours after he crossed us the first time. Besides, he knows he'll be taken care of so long as he follows orders so why should he try a double-cross?"

Hugh nodded. "That's what I wanted to hear," he said. "I was sorta scared you fellers might be too much the gentlemen to really play rough if you had to."

Pakenham grunted, "Ask some of the people who've tried to diddle us if we're too gentle—if you can find any alive."

"You mean you had 'em knocked off?" North asked. "Rubbed out?"

"Nothing quite so vulgar," Pakenham replied, with something close to a smile. "No, we've always found an *accidente del tráfico* more convenient than a gangland style job." He looked more carefully at Hugh and added: "An *accidente del tráfico* is—"

"Hell, I been dealin' with Mexicans 'most all my life," Hugh broke in breezily. "I know enough Spanish to understand you have 'em run down by a car."

Sir George Pakenham shrugged. "If you insist on putting it in words of one syllable," he sneered.

"Yahoo Gregory" gave his loud laugh. "You slay me, Dook," he said. "You knock off anybody that stands in the way of you earnin' a coupla bucks and then you don't like it when I put it in simple words."

"Now, Yahoo," Grafton broke in nervously, "we don't want to spend any more time than we have to on this. You've got the essential details. What do you say; are you in with us?"

Hugh North looked around the conference table, marking the urgency that lay in Grafton's eyes, the noncommittal look given him by Ward, the unfriendliness in Pakenham's stare.

"Hell, seems to me that when you told me what you're up to I was in whether I liked it or not," North said, grinning and tilting his sombrero back a trifle. "If I say no, I reckon there'll be one of them *accidente del tráficos* for me. My plane will be hit by lightning or my car will go haywire in the mountains or—well, I ain't foolin' myself any about what might happen if I pulled out of this deal, knowin' what I know."

Sir George Pakenham's voice was level and—to North—sincere. "You have my word that you can pull out now and nothing will happen to you," he told Hugh.

"Call me Yahoo," the colonel said. "And don't worry about me pullin' out; I'm in. But first I want to know what return I'd get on my investment. You told me the set-up—now, how much you figgerin' to ask me for to buy chips with in this game?"

"Eight million five hundred thousand," Townley Ward said quietly.

North did not bat an eyelash. G-2's information was that the last reportable figure on Yahoo Gregory's fortune was roughly three hundred and sixty million dollars, give or take a couple of million. Eight million, North told himself now, was a right nice little sum but not one which would have made the real Yahoo kick over the table and shoot out the lights.

"For that I get what kind of split?" he asked, as quietly as Townley had spoken.

"Quarter share," Grafton said hoarsely. "We're all in this even Stephen."

"Y'mean you're puttin' up eight-five?" North asked.

Grafton hesitated a second, then shook his head. "Not quite," he said. "I'm in for less because my organization did all the work of setting this up; this is my baby."

"And you, Dook?" North pursued, turning toward Pakenham. "What are you in for?"

"I could say it was my own business," the Englishman grated, "but I'll tell you—eight-five, the same as you, if you come in."

North nodded slowly, then drew a deep breath. "I don't want to look chinche, men," he told the others, "but I gotta go over some facks and figgers about this deal before I say yes or no. I'm past the day when I useta shake hands on a deal and take the other feller's word for it."

Wesley Grafton mopped his forehead with a handkerchief although the conference room was air-conditioned. "We expected you would," he said. He walked to a desk and opened a drawer, pulled out a heavy file folder. "Here's the proof you'll need, Yahoo. Go over it with a fine-tooth comb, if you like. You'll see we've got a great opportunity here."

North looked down at the folder and shook his head. "Hell, I ain't much at figgers," he said. "My secretary will have to go through these." He looked up at Grafton. "Don't s'pose there's a chance to fly these to my home office and have them look 'em over, is there?"

It was Sir George Pakenham who answered sharply. "Absolutely impossible," he snapped. "Matter of fact, I'm against their leaving this office, if you must know."

Hugh's inquiring gaze was puzzled. "What in hell could I do with 'em, stuck out here on an island the cops won't let me off?" he asked. "I got a pretty good idea you've got the telephone fixed so I can't spill anything to Salt Lake, either, so where's the danger?"

Pakenham shrugged his impeccably tailored shoulders with a twitch of impatience. "There are such things as cameras," he said. "Photographs of those documents would be extremely embarrassing if they got into the wrong hands before we were ready to make our move."

The pseudo Yahoo Gregory looked at the Englishman admiringly. "Damn if you don't think of everything," he said. "Imagine thinkin' I'd take snapshots of theseyere papers."

The big titled Britisher eyed North closely and then snorted. Hugh knew he was thinking of this Yahoo Gregory as the English equivalent of strictly bush league, not to have known about and dealt with such things as microfilm.

Hugh grinned at Ward and Grafton. "Tellya what—s'pose you go over my rooms and see if I got any kodaks hid around there anywhere." *Not that you haven't already gone through my things and missed the camera by six country miles.*

Ward said, "Don't be silly, Yahoo. You know we trust you or we wouldn't have invited you to sit in. Go ahead; take whatever papers you think you'll need to your rooms and go over them with your secretary. But let us have your answer as soon as you can, please. Sir George has this Kenya hunting trip lined up and I want to be in New York myself, as soon as I can."

"Don't rush him," Grafton protested. "Let him have all the time he needs."

"And don't forget Patricia," Hugh said. "Mebbe Boyd won't let us do any huntin' in Kenya—wherever that is—or anything else for a while. Speakin' of which, has Boyd found out who Patricia really was yet?"

Grafton shook his head. "No, but my bet is she was just a chiseler who read the death notices and moved in to try to get Judy's things. I understand they're fairly common; it's a well-known racket."

"This one sure-gawd didn't get nothin' but a busted neck," North said. He squinted at Pakenham. "You boys admit you play rough; did any of you have anything to do with Patricia's *accidente mortal, amigos?*"

Sir George's broad face reddened. "I was somewhere between here and Lisbon when it happened," he told North. "Of course I can't speak for the other two."

"Of course we didn't have anything to do with it," Grafton said peevishly. "Just what reason would we have to—"

"Now, Wes," Ward broke in hastily, "Yahoo was only kidding, I'm sure. He knows it was a real accident, regardless of Creepy's histrionics."

"If you mean boo-hooin' about murderin' Patricia, how about that?" the G-2 colonel marveled. "You figger he's just nuts?"

"Hard to figure these natives, Yahoo," Ward shrugged. "They're all scared to death of the police and they're liable to do or say anything when they panic. Creepy's possibly mixed up with something illegal in this Gombey business and—well, my only explanation is that he flipped his lid when Boyd came up with the wanga."

"Well, how did the wanga get there, then?" North asked.

"Hell, you'll find that native junk all around Freebooter's Hall," Grafton grumbled. "They're always putting crazy things around to keep out the evil spirits. That damned wanga might have been lying there in the quarry garden for weeks; nobody ever goes out there any more and hasn't since my first wife died."

Sir George Pakenham was tucking the fountain pen he had had no occasion to use into his pocket, pushing back his chair. "I suggest you forget all about that stupid accident and this native hysteria and concentrate on those papers, Gregory," he said rudely. "I want to get to Kenya on time and if you're not ready by the time I have to leave, the deal's off, that's all."

"No!" Grafton cried. "After all the work I've put in on this, we can't have it wrecked for a damned hunting trip."

"Sorry, Grafton," the Britisher said, "but I'm not in the habit of twiddling my thumbs, waiting for somebody else to make up his mind."

North looked down at the papers, scratched his head just under the sombrero's rim. "My secretary's an awful careful feller that goes over all the fine print twice," he said. "I'll need overnight, anyway."

"Perfectly all right," Townley Ward said swiftly as Pakenham seemed on the verge of speaking. "While you and your secretary are working, the three of us can go fishing, eh, Wes? There were a lot of sails working yesterday and they still might be out there."

"Who's gonna run the boat?" Hugh asked. "Creepy's still in the *calabozo*, ain't he? And is Boyd gonna let you go fishin'?"

"I told you not to concern yourself with anything but those papers," Pakenham graveled. "You'll need all your concentration on some of those figures—it's a little more than a case of simple addition and subtraction, y'know."

"Well, pardon me all to hell," North shot back. "What kinda bug you got in your ear, podner? Seems every time I try to be friendly, you come up with a nasty crack."

"No," Grafton said hoarsely. "He doesn't mean—"

"Well, lemme tell you somethin', Dook," the colonel plunged on as he gathered up the papers, "I been dealin' with tough *hombres* all my life—some mebbe even a little tougher than you—and I never been so scared yet that I threw my poke at their feet and run. I'll look over these papers and if I don't like what I see, or my secretary don't, I'm gonna stay outta this game. Maybe you can try to have an *accidente del tráfico* happen to me, but while you're tryin' make sure *you* don't cross on no red lights neither."

With which he started marching for the door. Wesley Grafton caught him before his hand touched the knob. "You mis-

understood Sir George," he cried. "We don't want to have
your feelings hurt, for God's sake. Come on, let's have a
drink."

"No," the G-2 man said with a decided headshake. "I gotta
concern myself with theseyere papers and their long division,
like the dook·said. Excuse me."

He left the conference room and stalked to his quarters in
the west wing. He told himself it was too bad that the opportunity had not presented itself to rig his own bug in that room
he had just left; he had the idea that there was a lot of interesting conversation going on.

He gained his room and knocked, was admitted by Kenny
Trotter. The young lieutenant gestured toward the desk where
the playing cards were scattered and grimaced. "Nothing," he
announced. "They must've been switched. How did you make
out?"

North hoisted the bundle of papers. "Get the Brownie un-
limbered," he grinned. "We've got some cute snapshots of the
kiddies to make for Aunt Ella."

Kenny nodded delightedly and went to the colonel's clothes
closet, emerging with one of "Yahoo Gregory's" most ornate
boots. A twist of Trotter's wrist and the high heel was de-
tached, revealing the eye of a lens. The aide held the heel
upside down and a tiny camera, a miracle of the minicam
maker's art, slid out. No bigger than a pullet egg, this marvel
of photography was capable of snapping pictures under almost any light conditions so sharply that when the negatives
were blown up by projection, the tiniest typewriter character-
istics stood out plainly, the slant and shading of handwriting
was made available to the experts' study.

Hugh North had told Pakenham and the others that he
would need hours to study the papers; actually, the G-2 colonel and his aide had everything photographed within half
an hour, the camera back in its boot heel, the damning evidence of international law violation, unscrupulous plotting,
indelibly recorded, ready for use by Uncle Sam's State Department, Justice Department, and whatever other agencies
might take a hand in slapping down these greedy men.

"If it wasn't for Judy Forthier and Patricia," Hugh North said as he replaced the boot in the closet, "we could haul out of here—I could tell that snotty Pakenham that I didn't think the partners were my clawss of people or something else gratifying."

"Do you think they'd let us reach the States if you pulled out?" Kenny asked.

The colonel shrugged. "I guess they'd try to keep us from getting there," he acknowledged. "Maybe they'd succeed, too —but that's one thing we don't have to worry about because we're not leaving until we find out what happened to Judy. Also, who Patricia was working for and who killed her and why."

"What's your guess on who sent her in here?" the aide asked curiously.

"Too early for that," Hugh grunted. "Right now I'd say Pakenham moved her in. His Insufferable Lordship doesn't give a damn whether this deal goes through or not—actually, I think he'd prefer to have it fall through because Yahoo Gregory withdrew. I don't know what angle he's playing, but whatever it is, it fits with Patricia's few words to me. She might have been trying to queer the deal by scaring Yahoo off with some scandal about a murdered girl." He sighed and added: "Pure conjecture, of course. The clerk will strike it out. I'm for a Scotch."

He had just finished mixing the drink and was enjoying his first sip when a knock sounded at the door. Both men swept the room with their eyes to make sure there was no evidence of their picture-taking; Kenny Trotter took the Scotch and soda from the bourbon-drinking "Yahoo Gregory," and then North nodded. Kenny went to the door, turned the night latch, and opened up.

"I know I'm a terrible nuisance, butting in like this," Sue Anne Pendleton said, "but can I speak to you a minute, Yahoo? It's right important."

[5]

"Come in, come in," Hugh cried. "And, Kenny, why don't you go for a nice long walk while I find out what the little lady wants of me?"

Trotter's reluctance to leave his chief was entirely genuine. "Perhaps you'd better explain to Miss Pendleton that I'm your confidential secretary," he said. "I'm sure anything she has to say—"

"I know I'm being silly," Sue Anne broke in, "but I'd rather talk to Yahoo alone, if you don't mind. I won't keep him long, I promise."

She fluttered her long lashes at Kenny and as the young man still hesitated, she cooed: "I 'clare, I think it's just wonderful how you look after Yahoo. But for goodness' sake, relax —I won't hurt him. He'll be safe enough with me."

"You go along, Kenny-boy," North hooted. "I reckon I can look after myself."

Trotter gave up and left the room. Sue Anne deftly snapped the night latch closed again and turned to smile at Hugh. She leaned back against the door and drew in a deep breath that brought into full prominence the breasts beneath the revealing cashmere sweater.

"I really didn't have anything so terribly important to talk to you about," she confessed. "I just wanted to see you alone for a few minutes. Aren't I awful?"

"Awful pretty," North countered. *Now, what the hell?* "And mighty flatterin' to an old man like me, too."

Sue Anne came slowly toward the colonel. "Old man!" she scoffed. "You're not fooling me one minute with that old man talk, Yahoo." She glanced over at the half-full Scotch that Kenny had deposited on a table near the door. "Have you got a little drinkie for me?" she asked.

"Before noon?" the colonel grinned. "Startin' in kinda early for a young girl, ain't you? It's all right for old mavericks like me to start loadin' up at sunrise but ain't you afraid you'll get tight before cocktail time, mebbe?"

"Would that be so terrible, if I was with you?" Sue Anne murmured, coming closer. "I know you'd look after me, wouldn't you?"

By this time she was so close that North could smell her delectable perfume, feel the animal heat of her young body. Sue Anne, he told himself clinically, was capable of stirring a mere male at twenty paces when she really turned it on. The girl knew this; she was supremely confident of her ability to get a man quiveringly avid whenever she chose—even at eleven o'clock in the morning.

Hugh played the game of flattered, bedazzled, salacious old goat. As Sue Anne gently undulated against him he put down a hand and patted her hip. "Y'know," he said huskily, "I could be awful nice to a young gal who was nice to me."

"But how could anybody help but be nice to you?" the girl from Georgia asked throatily. "You make all these other men seem so—so drippy. A girl gets tired of all this talking and hinting and no action, and that's about all you get from people like that Terry James. A girl needs somebody with more fire and life."

And dough, Colonel North added silently. Aloud, he said: "I been sort a waitin' for somethin' like this ever since I first set eyes on you, Sue Anne. First time I saw you I said to myself: 'Now there's a gal that the two of us could really go places, if she had a mind to.'"

Sue Anne Pendleton, as close to North as she could get now, looked up at him with enormous, humid blue eyes. "This gal has a mind to, Yahoo," she said softly. "What are you going to do about it?"

So there it was, the overt invitation, and what reason lay behind it? Colonel Hugh North had no exaggerated opinion of his qualifications as an Adonis, even under the best circumstances; as Yahoo Gregory he must appeal to an extremely limited circle of women of whom it was doubtful that Sue Anne was a dues-paying member. Still, North had been warned by a half-crocked Grafton that Sue Anne was a man-eater; perhaps she actually was a pathological case who took her men where she hunted them out and never mind·their looks or the hour of the day.

Grafton had said her family had gone broke; was Sue Anne ready to lay that gorgeous body on the line for money, a Park Avenue apartment, the modern-day counterpart of a sugar daddy?

The G-2 agent looked down into the blonde's melting eyes and gave a rueful laugh. "You pick the damnedest time to tell me this," he said. "You know Kenny ain't gonna hold still outside this room for long. We don't want anybody rappin' when we—ah—start to get acquainted, do we?"

"Tonight, then," Sue Anne breathed. "Barby says we're going to that Gombey dance tonight and there'll be a beach steak-out later. We can slip away."

"We sure can," North nodded enthusiastically, and then paused. "But how we gonna have any Gombey dance when Creepy's in the can?" he asked. "I thought he was the big wheel of the Gombeys."

The blonde nodded. "He is, but Inspector Boyd just brought him back," she said. "He told Barby that Creepy and all the rest of us had to stay close by but Creepy wasn't under arrest. He's going to talk to us all in a few minutes. Maybe"—she shivered in a motion that felt genuine to North's hand on her hip—"maybe he'll arrest somebody *else*."

"Hell, there ain't no reason to arrest nobody,". North scoffed. "Patricia just fell and Creepy—I reckon he wanted to see his name in the paper or some'n." He patted Sue Anne's flank again. "Just don't you worry your pretty head about it. It ain't got nothin' to do with us."

"No, 'course not." Sue Anne looked back over her shoulder at the door, then snuggled closer. "Well, if we can't depend on that secretary of yours not coming back in the middle of things, we'll have to wait 'til tonight, I reckon. So I'd better go. 'Til tonight, Yahoo."

She lifted her mouth to be kissed and Hugh bent his sombreroed head to oblige. It was a sizzler. The colonel had kissed many women, in line of duty and without, but seldom if ever

had he been kissed more thoroughly, more expertly, more de-
vouringly, with such cooperation from delectable parts of the
woman besides her mouth.

During the prolonged embrace, Hugh marveled at the girl's
recklessness, her lack of finesse. She must think Yahoo Gregory
a very direct-intentioned person, he told himself, if she could
be sure he wouldn't question such utter abandon on such short
acquaintance. Not that it wouldn't work on the average male,
he hastened to admit. Cool-thinking G-2 colonel he might be,
but at the end of the kiss he was almost as flustered as he
made himself appear.

"You don't have to go now," he muttered hoarsely. "We can
just let Kenny-boy rap his knuckles off."

"No, darling," Sue Anne whispered. "It'll be better tonight.
Then we can pay attention to what we're doing without being
afraid of somebody barging in."

"Okay, if you say so," North said sadly, and released the
delicious bundle of fragrant blonde. "But I dunno if I can wait
'til tonight or not."

"It won't be long," Sue Anne promised. She turned to go,
hesitated, and then turned back.

Here it comes.

"Oh, I forgot to tell you," Sue Anne said, with immense
afterthought. "I *do* have something to say to you, after all—
besides the other, I mean."

"Shoot," North invited.

"Well, Barby—she's my best friend, you know—we were
down on the pier watching Stan Gibbons' boat come in and
Barby said that if Inspector Boyd ever got off his—I mean if
he really worked at his job, he might find something interesting on Stan Gibbons' boat. It just sort of slipped out and she
wouldn't tell me any more but—well, I wondered if I ought to
tell Inspector Boyd?"

"I wouldn't," Hugh North said promptly. "Not right away,
anyway. If I was you, I wouldn't say nothin' that might get
you mixed up in this mess."

"No, lordy—I don't want to do that."

"Then you just leave it to old Yahoo," the colonel said. "I'll get word to the inspector about Gibbons' boat—after I see which way the wind's blowin'."

5.

[1]

KENNY KNOCKED then and a few minutes later Sue Anne was gone. The colonel's aide had to give the girl from Georgia a stern, chilly frown in his role of secretary to Yahoo Gregory, but Hugh North could see the yearning in the lieutenant's eyes. Trotter waited only until the girl's steps receded down the hallway before he turned on his colonel.

"Look at you," he said in disgust. "Lipstick from ear to ear and the sweat's dripping off you. Your forehead—hey, what about your sombrero?"

North whirled toward a mirror, stared, and simultaneously cursed and grinned. During Sue Anne's kiss, Hugh had dropped his guard, as what mortal man would not have? And Sue Anne, either accidentally or by design, had used her neck-wrapping clutch to tilt his ever-present sombrero back until half North's crown was exposed.

The colonel spoke aloud, slowly and solemnly. "I thought they were going a little too far at headquarters when they shaved me a bald head to match Yahoo's," he said, "but now I know they were wiser than I ever hope to be."

He took off his sombrero and studied the tonsorial master-piece that G-2 had achieved. His dome was bald, as the real Yahoo's was, except for a fringe just under the hatband's ridged mark. If Sue Anne Pendleton had launched herself upon Hugh North with the purpose of finding out if he were truly the bald Yahoo, she must be convinced he was. G-2's careful planning had paid off.

But if this had been deliberate, why had Sue Anne bothered? Of all these people on Plunder Island, was the big-breasted blonde the one who suspected that Yahoo Gregory was not the McCoy? Did she have orders to make sure, one way or the other?

"Why do you frown, effendi?" Kenny Trotter asked.

Hugh laughed wryly. "I'm busy making up trouble," he explained. "The sombrero merely got tilted back in the heat of events."

"A wisely chosen word, heat," Kenny snickered. "Go wash your face and while you soap away your marks of shame I'll tell you my news. While you were grappling with the fair Sue Anne, I was *working.*" He held up a hand. "Oh, no, Mr. Dithers, no hand-kissing, please. I *like* to work. I'd rather work than rassle with delicious blondes. When you retire—is it this year or next?—I'll show G-2 what a man—"

"Will you shut up and get on with it?" North gritted.

"Okay," Kenny said in a hurt voice. "Here 'tis. Item: Boyd is back from Hamilton with three or four constables besides Lunt. He's still playing it like a man who needs sleep. They must have run the autopsy, but he's not saying a word about that breast wound. Item: Creepy went back behind the wheel of *Amphitrite* just as though he never heard of a wanga. Item: Pakenham, Ward, and our host started out on said *Amphitrite* to troll for sailfish, but the word is that they radio-phoned in that they had engine trouble and please pick them up. Item: one of the new constables went out in the patrol launch to pick up Pakenham, Ward, and Grafton and also to tell Stan Gibbons to move his ketch around from Hidden Bay to the pier out front, request of the drooping Inspector Boyd."

"Then Gibbons was close by when Patricia was killed."

"By dint of some pretty neat eavesdropping, if I do say it myself, I heard Gail deny that hotly. Said Stan left Hidden Bay when she started for Freebooter's Hall last night to join you on the pier and went offshore to sleep, was due to come back to Hidden Bay this morning."

"I don't suppose anybody will be able to prove differently," North said.

"Boyd doesn't suppose so, either," the lieutenant offered. "I overheard him ask Barbara Grafton if she had any way of knowing whether Gibbons was or was not in Hidden Bay all night and she said no, but if Gibbons said he wasn't, he was. Said Gibbons couldn't be believed on a stack of Bibles, King James version."

"Gibbons isn't Barbara's favorite boy," North smiled.

"Nor Grafton's," Kenny added. "You've got to hand it to the guy—he sticks in there against some pretty formidable opposition from the Graftons, *père et belle mère.*"

Hugh stood at the wash basin, removing Sue Anne's lipstick imprints. He said over his bent shoulder: "So our theory might still stand about Creepy seeing Gail coming back from a tryst on Gibbons' boat and trying to protect her."

"It does if Barbara isn't just using the knife on Gibbons out of habit," the lieutenant offered.

"There's that, too. I get the distinct impression that Barbara is not fond of Gail." Hugh hesitated a long moment and then added: "Nor of Gail's father."

"Her husband?" Kenny asked with a stare into the mirror over North's shoulder.

"Maybe I'm wrong," the G-2 colonel admitted, "but I think that while Grafton is crazy about his new wife, the fair Barbara's already fed up with the man she divorced a perfectly good—though not as rich—husband to get. You weren't on the pier last night when she said she was bored to death, sitting in the most romantic setting on earth and listening to nothing but business, business, business."

"Did Grafton raise hell about that?"

"He wasn't there, but I don't think it would have made much difference to Barbara if he had been. I think that's one of the reasons Grafton's drinking so heavily—I doubt he'd get plastered on the eve of a big deal unless he had something pretty wormy on his mind. It could be that he's worried about losing Barbara."

"How about his being worried over Judy Forthier's death?"

Hugh nodded. "Sure he is. Also the suicide note—he may know that's a phoney."

"But if he knew it was no suicide, why did he plant Judy's clothes on the beach to cover up?"

"He may have thought he had to make the accidental swimming death convincing," Colonel North explained. "An accident was bad enough, with Yahoo Gregory due to arrive—a suicide and the papers would holler loud enough to be heard in Salt Lake and Yahoo might stay put."

The G-2 agent toweled his face and wondered absently just how long it would take for the high-blood-pressure dye to work out of his pores. "It could even be that Grafton knows who killed Judy. He might have done it himself—or Ward."

"I thought you said it would have been more logical for Grafton and Townley to kick Judy out if they found her spying on them," Trotter reminded his chief.

"That was before I heard them talking about *accidentes del tráfico*," Hugh said. "Liquidating meddlers by accidental death seems to be Standard Operating Procedure with this bunch. Maybe Judy did get enough information to sign her death warrant, after all."

He refitted the sombrero to his head and peered into the bathroom glass. "I've got to phone Salt Lake again," he told Kenny. "No better time than now, with Grafton, Ward, and Pakenham out fishing."

He moved to the telephone, lifted the receiver.

". . . nothing to make an arrest on, sir," he heard Inspector Boyd tell somebody on the other end of the line. The inspector stopped abruptly, conscious of somebody listening in, and then said mildly: "Hullo, hullo? Mind getting off the wire, please? Police business here."

"Excuse me, podner," Hugh North boomed in his best Yahoo voice. "Didn't know the line was busy." He hung up the receiver with a clatter, signaling Kenny Trotter by a gesture even as he replaced the phone in its cradle.

The lieutenant hurried to the attaché case, slid out its false bottom compartment to extract the tiniest wire-tapping outfit yet devised by G-2 laboratories. Wire and earplug, cut-in clamps and all, the thing barely weighed two ounces and could have been packed in a matchbox. Kenny deftly applied the clamps that sank their needle-sharp teeth through the phone cord's insulation to the copper conductor while North fitted the earplug.

". . . Cavendish [that was Creepy] won't talk, though we all know he's hiding something."

"Be sure you watch him sharply," the other voice, a brusque, official voice Hugh had never heard before, said.

"Oh, indeed I will," Boyd promised. "I'm watching all of them, actually. Especially this fantastic chap, Yahoo Gregory."

Well, now!

Boyd asked: "Did anything come from C.I.D. on Gregory, sir? You said when I was there that you expected—"

"Yes, yes; just came through. C.I.D.'s people in Washington say he checks out all right. Fantastic is the word for Gregory but they say he is in Bermuda, the guest of Wesley Grafton. It would be enormously difficult for him *not* to be Gregory, they say; there seems to be only one of that type in the whole wide world."

Hugh North grinned.

There was a silence on the line and then Boyd's superior said: "Well, carry on, Inspector. I'm trusting to your judgment in letting these people walk about instead of finding some charge to get at least the prime suspects out of circulation. Can't have another murder over there, y'know. One's quite enough."

One? Then the Bermuda police are writing off Judy Forthier?

The colonel asked himself whether this man, Boyd, really was the ineffectual he seemed. North had heard and read of indolent young geniuses, British police inspectors or dilettante detectives, who hid their rattrap minds beneath a vacuous mask but he had never met one—he was willing to bet they didn't exist. Or was Inspector Boyd a living specimen of this rare, if not entirely legendary, breed that had all been fathered by Sherlock Holmes?

"Oh, I quite agree," Boyd was saying, "but on the other hand we don't want another Oakes mess by too hasty action, I take it."·

"Decidedly not!" The other's voice was emphatic and Colonel North could understand why; the murder of the millionaire Sir Harry Oakes was a case that had dragged on for a decade, a thorn in the flesh to Nassau authorities close by— and ostensibly all because of hasty police work at the beginning.

"What about Stanley G.?" the heavier voice on the wire asked.

Stan Gibbons. Yes, what about him?

"You were quite right, sir; he doesn't pay his gambling debts with what he gets for his papers and pictures on fish life. Somebody's furnishing him with a great deal of money, and when we find out who it is we may get somewhere. I'm questioning him and all the others after lunch."

Another brief silence and then Boyd's superior said: "All right, carry on. Call on Hamilton for anything you need. Keep in touch."

"Yes, sir. Thank you, sir. Good-by, sir."

Receivers clattered and the line went dead. Hugh North disengaged the wire tap, frowning slightly. Was this the way the Bermuda authorities worked, over a phone that even Boyd must realize was an invitation to eavesdropping? Or had Boyd possibly staged this conversation to spread false assurances?

The colonel lifted the phone again, after a decent interval, and found the line open. He put through a reverse call to Salt Lake City, confident that Grafton's (or the triumvirate's) ear —probably Terry James—was listening in, and spoke at some length again with "George L. Van Huse." When he was through, the G-2 man knew that the ambitious Colonel Guerra was due an early and unpleasant surprise. Paratina being the impulsive little country it was, it was not at all impossible that Guerra would find himself backed up against an adobe wall, smoking the traditional last cigarette, before nightfall.

North had only a slight twinge of sympathy for his fellow colonel. While he admitted that South and Central American army officers might have a different code of ethics from West Pointers, he felt the venal colonel who could start a revolution and wreck his country for the gold he could stuff into his pockets before the roof fell in had it coming to him.

So much, then, for the revolution-for-profit angles to this case. Now to find Judy Forthier's murderer and bring him or her to justice. Judy had been a United States undercover agent and as such her killer would have to be hunted down at all costs. Then, too, Patricia's case needed solving; apparently she had been murdered because she had worked, or had come close to working, the playing-card code message left behind by Judy Forthier and now in the hands of Patricia's killer and very likely Judy's.

"Now," Hugh told Kenny as he left the chair he had used for his phone call, "let's see about lunch, and Boyd's little session."

The two G-2 men left their room after planting several almost invisible markers to signal intruders and went to the main living quarters of Freebooter's Hall. They found the big living room empty and went to the veranda to be greeted by empty chairs there.

"See if you can rustle up some grub, podner," North boomed. "My belly tells me it's feedin' time and I could do with a drink, too, if you pass a bottle of bourbon on your way."

"Yes, sir," said Kenny and departed in search of somebody to direct him toward food and whiskey. North stood at the top of the front steps, his hands on his hips, looking out over the harbor of Plunder Island with the hulk of King's Castle looming to the south. It was a beautiful Bermuda day with the sun sparkling on the water, a light wind stirring the waves into tiny whitecaps. Gulls and terns swooped and wheeled; out beyond the harbor entrance a small school of porpoises showed their glistening backs as they arched past. A pair of man-o'-war birds soared high above the castle tower, their wings motionless, and beneath them passed a "V" of pelicans in their squadron formation.

North inhaled deeply, relishing the winey air, wishing briefly that some day his job would let him enjoy surroundings like these without the pall of murder and hate hanging heavy. His job had carried Hugh to some of the most spectacularly beautiful spots on earth and almost never had the G-2 colonel been able to relax and enjoy himself; always there had been some killer to catch, some enemy agent to outwit, some foul plot to be wrecked.

There was no sign of *Amphitrite* but the police launch was in a slip of the Freebooter's Hall pier and another, larger boat was moored some distance out. This was a graceful white ketch of about sixty feet, her sails neatly furled, her hull rocking gently. North knew it must be Stan Gibbons' boat, the craft that Gail Grafton did or did not visit when she was supposed to be in her own bed.

A dinghy bobbed beside the pier, next to the police launch, and North left the veranda and moved down the shell walk. A newly rich uranium man from Utah, he told himself, could hardly be expected to know that to board another man's boat uninvited and with the owner absent was the nadir of bad manners, and he wanted to find out if Barbara Grafton's alleged slip of the tongue that Sue Anne overheard had anything to it—if, indeed, Barbara had ever said any such thing.

He found stubby oars in the dinghy, cast free the mooring line, and made his way to the ketch. A ladder hung from the lee side—"*Porifera of Hamilton*," the legend on the stern read —and North tied up the dinghy, went up the ladder.

"Anybody home?" he called when he gained the deck. His only answer came from the subdued creaking of the idle boom, swinging in time to the boat's motion.

North saw the hatch that led below and clanked his high-heeled boots toward the opening, wincing inwardly at the thought of what those leather heels would do to this splendid teak deck. He had taken half a dozen steps when something slammed the side of his head and everything went black.

[2]

Colonel North lay unconscious on the deck of the ketch *Porifera* for eleven minutes but it seemed a decade, an eon, later when he struggled up out of the dark pit of oblivion to find the Bermuda sun scorching his lids.

He struggled to a sitting position, choking back a groan, and forced his eyes open despite the pain caused by the water's glare. The G-2 colonel discovered that he had fallen behind the top of the cabin raised a foot or so above the main deck and had thus effectively shielded himself from anyone ashore. This had prevented Kenny from finding him—and at the same time had kept the sniper from taking a second shot, a *coup de grâce,* at his leisure.

For Hugh North found out soon enough that it had been a bullet that had felled him. A hand touched gingerly to the side of his head just under the ridge left by the sombrero's hatband came away bloody after its fingertips traced a short groove in the skin a half an inch above the eyebrow. By a hairsbreadth, the slug had missed ending the career of Colonel Hugh North, U.S. Army, G-2.

"Creepy's an expert with the .22," North muttered, "but his specialty is night sniping. Perhaps that's what saved my life; Creepy has owl eyes and he's terrible in daylight—off target a sixteenth of an inch at a hundred yards."

Wincing, the colonel got to his hands and knees, peered shoreward over the cabin top. His wrist watch showed him the time, and he knew the gunman could hardly have waited around this long for another shot; it was safe enough to at least peep at Freebooter's Hall. The deck whirled briefly under him in his giddiness, and he shut his eyes again until the seascape stopped revolving; then he scanned the big house and the shore.

Freebooter's Hall was quiet with no one in sight except a gardener who worked in the profusion of flowers at the end of the east wing, a crouched figure shielded by an enormous straw hat. Creepy? Did the skipper of *Amphitrite* also double as gardener, besides acting as rat-hunter of Plunder Island?

No, Kenny had said that Ward, Pakenham, and Grafton were out after sailfish aboard *Amphitrite* and Creepy must be at the wheel of the cruiser. Which, if that proved true, removed four men as those who could have fired that shot at "Yahoo Gregory."

"Wonder if that bullet's around anywhere?" the G-2 man muttered aloud.

It was an odds-on chance that the slug had zinged on past North after creasing him, to drop into the water beyond the ketch, but the colonel's search was thorough, nonetheless. And it paid off: the minute deflection in the slug's trajectory caused by its collision with Hugh's hard skull apparently had been enough to slant it off plunk into the mainmast amidships. The spent bullet had not buried itself deeply; it required only a few seconds for the G-2 agent to dig it out with his knife.

It was a .22 slug, one that could have been fired by the rifle North had seen in Creepy's capable hands behind Freebooter's Hall near midnight.

North looked hard at that gardener. As he watched, the man worked his way around a corner of the big house and was lost to view.

Hugh touched his wound again and found the blood clotting well; it could go without sterilizing for the few minutes it would take him to give this ketch a going-over. The colonel moved to the hatch, found it padlocked, and used one of his keys to throw it open.

He descended to a cabin that was the perfect example of tidy seamanship and prim living. Stan Gibbons was that unusual bachelor who did not fling his clothes about or leave dirty dishes in the galley. Everything was in order, even in the tiny laboratory that took up part of the living space—a letdown counter on which sat labeled jars and bottles, set in clamps that kept them from shifting with the motion of the ketch.

The colonel ignored the laboratory counter and made for a foot locker under the tautly sheeted bunk. This proved locked, necessitating the use of another of Hugh's master keys before the lid went back.

Besides being a shipshape boatman, Stan Gibbons obviously was an extremely careful young man—either that, or he had his more interesting gear stowed elsewhere on *Porifera* or ashore. The ketch's log revealed no more than the state of wind and weather, knots and miles, anchorages visited, catches and photographs made, on the days set forth. There were no diary, no snapshots except of fish life, no bankbooks, checkbook stubs, letters, except from museums and other ichthyologists (stuffy crowd by their correspondence), or even a postcard dealing with Stan Gibbons' private life.

Inspector Boyd had mentioned Gibbons' gambling debts; surely this was the strangest gambler North had ever met up with. Usually, addicts of the wheel, the dice, the pasteboards, let their compulsion show through in their private life; from what Hugh North was able to find in this cabin, Stan Gibbons might have been a dry-as-dust scientist with no interests except his calling, the study of marine life.

North replaced the foot locker, his frown showing his disappointment. He had not known what he expected to find—indeed, he had placed very little faith in Sue Anne's tip—but after having been shot at and almost killed for having dared board the ketch, it seemed to him that his search should have been rewarded a little more generously.

He gave a final look around. Time was growing short; he had been lucky to have been given all these minutes without somebody discovering the gig's disappearance, without Gibbons wanting back on his ketch. *Where would I hide anything if this were my boat?*

The usual hiding places found in a dwelling did not apply here. There was no possibility of a wall safe; there were no pictures on the bulkheads behind which to hide anything. Even the toilet in the head had no water tank, that hideaway for alcoholics since the invention of the bottle. There were, however, hiding places on a boat that were not available ashore, the rope locker (North drew a blank there), the bilge —ah, the bilge.

He left the cabin, replaced the padlock, and examined the ketch's cockpit. Stan Gibbons was a true sailing man; the engine he carried was the smallest that could move a craft this size and the opening to the bilge was comparatively tiny. Hugh knelt and groped about in the damp, smelly beneath-decks cavity—and struck paydirt almost at once. His fingers touched an oilskin bag, attached to the underside of the cockpit deck by an ingenious arrangement of clamps such as secured the bottles and jars on the laboratory bench.

The colonel spared a moment to glance shoreward. Still no signs of activity about Freebooter's Hall; even the gardener was still out of sight. North brought the waterproofed bag up on deck, unfastened the drawstring. As he examined the sack's contents he looked upon the ugly secret life of Stanley Gibbons.

Here were letters, plenty of them, mostly addressed in a feminine hand. There were pictures here, too, and negatives that made Hugh's stomach churn with disgust. North had seen his share of pornography in the course of his duties and until now he had considered the Orient as the worst source of salacious photographic "art," but now he revised his opinion; these unspeakable prints and negatives had plainly been made in the Bermudas, and yet they eclipsed in sheer viciousness anything he had ever seen.

The subjects in the photos that North studied clinically were all young women of a type seldom found pictured in such filth. They all bore the same look—a vacant stare not usually associated with such activities—and to the G-2 colonel that fact spelled one thing, the use of aphrodisiacs on unsuspecting girls for the purposes that had resulted in this foul collection.

"Boyd wants to know where Gibbons gets his money?" North murmured. "I think I can tell him. Blackmail."

To substantiate this theory was a red leather notebook containing a list of girls' names, some carrying the notation "Married." Opposite these names were some amounts that made Hugh North whistle softly. These were wealthy women, these victims of Stan Gibbons, and the "ichthyologist" was getting top prices in his evil, bloodsucking trade.

Hugh put the notebook in his pocket and went on with his search. And found evidence to support Boyd's mention of Stan's gambling debts. Another notebook contained a roulette system, a third was filled by figures with marginal notes explaining the dates and places where so much was won, so much lost—usually lost. There were three pairs of capped dice, six packs of marked cards.

Colonel Hugh North gave a grunt deep in his throat. There was a seventh pack of cards in Stan Gibbons' collection. It was not marked in the usual sense of the word but in another way it surely was. When the colonel pulled the pasteboards from their cardboard container he found one side of the pack scored by some sharp implement, manicure scissors or a nail file's point.

These were the cards Judy Forthier must have left behind her when she disappeared. These were the playing cards Patricia apparently had been trying to decipher when she was killed. These were the cards the murderer had taken when he or she had left behind the switched deck.

[3]

"What happened to you?" Kenny Trotter demanded plaintively. "When I came back to the veranda after finding the others you were gone. Don't tell me you holed up somewhere with Sue Anne and—hey, your head!"

Hugh finished painting his wound with a colorless cauterizing agent and bent to the tiny make-up kit that was another component of the attaché case's invaluable hidden compartment.

"Somebody took a shot at me," he explained briefly. "Who were the others you found when you left me on the veranda?"

"Who sho, vou?"

"Later. Who was here when you went to hunt up lunch?"

Trotter bit back his curiosity over the head wound, the result of long training. "Everybody," he said. "Barbara, Sue Anne, Gail, this guy Gibbons, Terry James, Pakenham, Grafton—"

North swung away from the mirror. "They were here? I thought they went fishing—oh, they broke down, didn't they?"

"Uh-huh," the lieutenant nodded. "Developed engine trouble the other side of the island. When the police went for Gibbons, they put Ward, Pakenham, and Grafton aboard Gibbons' ketch and brought 'em all in together. Must have been a merry party—all three despise Gibbons, from the looks of things."

"And Creepy, did they bring him, too?"

"No. I suppose they left him with the disabled boat."

"Never suppose, Lieutenant," North said severely. "And even if they did, he could land, trot across the island to take a pot shot at me, and be back with the cruiser before anybody knew he'd left it. How long did you stay with the crowd and where were they, by the way?"

"Out in back, in the *lanai*—or whatever they call 'em in Bermuda. I didn't stay but a few minutes. I started back right away to get you and when you weren't on the porch I went to our rooms and waited there, expecting you to come there. Then I hunted for you awhile around the grounds before I rejoined the folks on the *lanai*."

"Anybody ask after me when you came back without me?"

"Oh, yes, they all did. I didn't know what you'd want me to say so I stalled them—convincingly, I hope. Now can you tell me about that head of yours?"

North finished filling in the sterilized wound with a plastic which was textured to exactly copy the pore content of North's own skin. This he colored with a dye that made the patchwork absolutely invisible and which would keep the covered wound hidden in spite of water, heat, or even strenuous rubbing.

"I was out on Gibbons' boat," he explained, repacking the utensils he had used. "I'd just boarded her when somebody got me alongside the head. Good shooting; it must have been at least a hundred yards from the closest shore point."

"Didn't you get a look at the gunman?"

"No, I was knocked out. Down for about ten minutes. When I came to, I went through the ketch. I figured that whoever shot me might think he or she killed me and there'd be time before my body was discovered to give Stan's boat a shakedown."

"Find anything?"

"Plenty. Most important was the deck of cards Judy Forthier left behind."

"Hot dog!" Kenny exulted. "Then we've got our man!"

North shook his head glumly as he pushed an arm into the sleeve of the purple and gold double-breasted shirt. "No such luck," he gloomed. "Judy hadn't finished when she was interrupted."

"Oh, no!"

"Oh, yes! I just got through arranging the cards, using the code in that letter. Take a look."

Kenny hurried to the desk by the window and picked up the deck, examined its scored edge. All that showed, even though it was dug deeply into the serried edge, was: PARA-TINA. GUERRA. IF KILLED IT'S . . .

And that was all.

Trotter put down the cards with a curse. "Of all the stinking luck. If Judy'd just had a couple of seconds more—"

"She knew she didn't have any time. That's why she used that moth-eaten code in the first place. She was backed into a corner. She knew they were coming for her and the cards were handy so she put down the vital information, Paratina and Guerra, before she tried to name the one closing in on her."

"If she'd only reversed it," Trotter said in a subdued voice, and then shook his head. "I guess none of us would have in the same situation, though."

There was a brief silence as Hugh finished donning his Yahoo Gregory regalia. "Find anything else?" the lieutenant asked his colonel, to break the stillness.

"This Gibbons is a louse—a feelthy picture racketeer and blackmailer. Not even a shabby, greasy character who goes around pinching little girls; he poses as a prim and proper scientist and somehow that's even more indecent."

"Wesley Grafton will be glad to hear that," Kenny said. "It'll convince Gail that she shouldn't marry Gibbons. If Gibbons is going to be around to marry anybody, that is. I should think that when we give Boyd these cards and explain, it ought to wrap Stan Gibbons up pretty tight."

"Maybe," North said without any visible enthusiasm.

Kenny Trotter knew the signs. "In other words, you're not going to tell Boyd about your discoveries? You don't think Gibbons is our man?"

Hugh shook his head reluctantly. "No, I don't."

"Is one permitted to inquire why not?" the lieutenant asked.

"One is. And the reason may sound pretty feeble to you. But what's Gibbons' possible motive in killing Judy Forthier? The immediate answer is that he's in somebody's pay, somebody with a stake in this Paratina thing. Well, whose? And how could he earn his pay? I doubt like hell he's a professional gunman called in to dispose of Judy. He was *persona non grata* here at Freebooter's Hall until Inspector Boyd requested his presence. Wesley Grafton hates his guts. Was Gibbons likely to get any information out of him?"

"But didn't you tell me Grafton said he noticed Stan Gibbons fooling around with Judy when Gail wasn't looking? That indicates he was a guest here, at least."

"Oh, he probably was," North nodded, "but being an unwelcome guest would hardly qualify him to find out anything about a supersecret deal like the Paratina plot. Of course he might have been pumping Gail, but just how much does the girl know about her father's business?"

Kenny pursed his mouth, stroked his chin. "How's this?" he asked. "Suppose Gibbons is Barbara Grafton's boyfriend 'way over on the side, and he's been getting Paratina information through her while both of them put up a front about despising each other?"

"It's always possible, of course," North admitted. He donned the sombrero, hiding his wince as the sweatband pressed down on his recently cauterized wound. "Or Barbara could have hired him to work for her."

"Barbara?" Trotter's voice showed surprise.

"I'm beginning to think that Barbara had a big stake in the Paratina deal," Hugh said. "By the way Grafton acts, if this deal is a bust—and it is, of course—he's going to find the going rough, financially. If Barbara knows this, and she looks like the kind who should know what's going on, she'd be damned interested in keeping Judy Forthier from wrecking the deal."

"To the point of murdering Judy?" Trotter asked skeptically.

"I don't know," North admitted. He headed for the door. "Let's play it by ear for a while," he said. "Shall we join the others, Kenny-boy?"

"When this case is finished," Lieutenant Trotter said evenly, "and you call me Kenny-boy just once, I am going to face a general court-martial for busting a chicken colonel right in the nose—sir."

The people Trotter had mentioned were still in the *lanai*, dawdling over the remains of their lunch. North swaggered into the circle, loud-voiced and insufferable, and made for the portable bar at one side of the patio.

"I can use this." he boomed. "I been out gettin' some exercise and fresh air." He looked back at Grafton. "Thought you was goin' fishin'."

"The engine broke down," Townley Ward said cheerfully. "Rotten luck, too—I spotted two sails while we were drifting."

"Hell," cried North, pouring bourbon, "if I paid a man to look after my boat he better hadn't have no breakdowns. What kind of skipper you got, anyway, Grafton?"

"It couldn't have been Creepy's fault," Gail Grafton flared before her father could speak.

"Oh, God, no," Barbara Grafton murmured cynically. "Creepy can do no wrong."

There was an awkward pause. North swigged at his drink, then looked at the young man sitting beside Gail, the man who must be Stan Gibbons. Despite the fact that he had prepared himself for something like this, Hugh felt a shock at sight of the pornography photographer, the blackmailer. Stan Gibbons was a very handsome, very clean-cut young man, a sport-shirt model if Hugh had ever seen one. He was above average height with the shoulders of an oarsman, the healthy tan of the clean-living man, the smile of one perfectly at ease with the world and a friend to all.

As North looked at him, Gail's beloved rose from his chair and extended a hand. "I'm Stan Gibbons, Mr. Gregory," he said. "A pleasure to meet you, sir."

"Call me Yahoo," North directed and summoned a sheepish grin. "I think I got an apology to make to you, Stan. My secretary here tells me it ain't good manners to climb on anybody's boat when the owner's not there."

For a split second, Gibbons came close to losing his well-balanced aplomb. His eyes steeled and the smile grew rigid, the color beneath the heavy tan grayed a little before the young man recovered himself.

"Well, if your secretary feels an invitation was needed let me extend one now, Yahoo," he said. "Welcome aboard."

North nodded. "Thanks," he said. He turned away from Gibbons to sweep the circle with bland, all-seeing eyes. Which one of these people was fighting hysteria at seeing him standing there, apparently undamaged, talking calmly about having paid an uninvited visit to Stan Gibbons' ketch, where he should be lying dead?

Barbara's eyes were—was *watchful* the word?—as she stared at him. Her husband's answering look told North only that Wesley Grafton had been drinking again. Pakenham's eyes were as cold and contemptuous as ever. Townley Ward appeared a trifle embarrassed for Yahoo's sake over the trespassing blunder but nothing more. Terry James was grinning, sardonically or otherwise. Gail Grafton was looking up at Stan, her mouth curved in a smile and her eyes adoring. Sue Anne Pendleton had her nose buried in a tall glass of iced tea.

Here we have an actor or actress who can give Muni or Hayes pointers. Unless, of course, it was Creepy.

"Afraid I got a lot to learn about boatin' manners," the G-2 colonel went on. "Where I come from the doors are never locked and I s'posed it was the same way with boats."

"One usually stays off unless the Owner Aboard flag is flying," Sir George Pakenham said icily.

"Hell, I wouldn't know one if I saw one," Hugh said breezily. "Anyway, when I saw the padlock on the door to the whatchacallit, I got the point." He turned back to Gibbons.

"Used your rowboat, too," he added. "Shoulda seen me tryin'
to row with them little oars."

Gibbons turned to Gail. "Mind if I check to see if Yahoo
tied the dinghy up properly?" he asked.

"Hell, Kenny can do that," North boomed. He told Trotter: "Run down and see if I made the proper knot in the rope
on that rowboat."

"No, no," Gibbons protested, "I'll do it. Matter of fact, I've
got some things to do on the ketch before Inspector Boyd calls
his little party at two. Good-by, all. Thanks for the lunch."
The young ichthyologist-blackmailer headed for the pier, his
long stride hurried.

*And what are you going to do when you find those cards
missing?* North asked silently. *Try to make a bolt for it? You
won't get far, my friend.*

He sat down in the chair Gibbons had vacated, took another swallow of his drink. "Didn't mean to run your boyfriend off," he said. "Will I do as a substitute, maybe?"

"Now, that's not nice," Sue Anne cried from across the
circle. "I thought you were *my* boyfriend."

Barbara Grafton's lip curled faintly. "Mr. Gregory is probably confident that he can handle two, Sue Anne," she said.
"Wouldn't you like some lunch, Mr. Gregory?"

"That I do," North said, lurching out of his chair again,
"and don't let this beat-up face fool you, Barby. There's life
in the old dog yet, as the feller sez."

"What feller is this you're always quoting?" Terry James
asked.

"The feller that says young squirts oughta be seen and not
heard," North returned and made his way to the serving
table. It was a tempting buffet and Hugh heaped his plate
with crayfish and avocado salad, broiled red snapper, and a
helping of delicious (although faintly soggy, by this time)
chicken-liver omelet.

"This'll do for a starter," he said and seated himself beside
Gail with his plate on his lap. He chomped lustily for a moment, then called across to Grafton. "Mebbe I'll go fishin' with
you next time. I ain't much of a fisherman, though—huntin's

my sport. You have any huntin' in Bermuda? Besides rats, I mean?"

The sodden-faced millionaire said: "I understand they get ducks on certain parts of the islands but we don't do any shooting here except at targets. We save the wing shooting and such for when we're living in the States—I've got a place in Georgia for birds and another in Montana for big game."

"That's my sport," North enthused. "Pretty good at it, too, if I do say it myself who shouldn't. Pretty good on targets. Bet I can beat anybody here if they was to make it interestin'."

He stuffed his mouth with an overloaded fork.

"I'd be a bit careful about making wild bets, if I were you," Sir George Pakenham said disdainfully. "I happen to have done a bit of shooting, myself. When the target's a charging water buffalo, one can't afford to be only pretty good."

Barbara said, "As far as that goes, Wes is a good shot, I understand, and so is Townley. Creepy taught Gail to shoot when she was a little girl, I hear. Terry used to be good— are you still, brother mine?"

James shrugged. "Haven't had a gun in my hands for years," he said. "Probably couldn't hit the broad side of a barn."

"I'm scared of guns," Sue Anne offered. "They give me goose pimples just to touch one."

Gail stood up and arched her shoulders in a stretching shrug. "Well, don't anybody get a bet started that will have you all popping away with rifles, please. I intend to take a nap until Boyd's little party."

"I'm with you," Sue Anne said, and rose. "I was planning to go to St. George's and do some shopping, but now the boat's broken so I don't suppose I can."

"Even if the boat was all right, there's Boyd's get-acquainted party," Gail reminded the blonde. The dark-haired girl's face sobered. "He seems to have something on his mind ever since he brought Creepy back. Did he tell you anything when you asked him if it was all right to go fishing, Daddy?"

"No, just said he expected us to stay around Plunder Island and be back by two," Grafton replied. "Of course we got back a lot sooner, as it happened. And what do you mean, Boyd's got something on his mind? Of course he has—Patricïa and her accident and who she really was."

"I know but—oh, I'm just nerved up, I guess, but it seems as though he's holding something back. Something we're not going to like when he comes out with it."

"It was what Creepy did, the fool!" Barbara burst out, suddenly vehement. "What in the world got into him, making that ridiculous confession? If it hadn't been for that the police wouldn't have given the accident a second thought."

"Hardly that, Barbara," Townley Ward said smoothly. "Boyd knew Patricia was an impostor, remember. He'd have had to look into that. As to why Creepy told the story about the wanga, you've got me. No explaining these natives, sometimes."

"I got it all figgered out," Hugh put in, speaking through another mouthful. "This Patricia dame, she was really the other gal's long-lost sister nobody knew about. She didn't like the drownin' story, and she was snoopin' around tryin' to be the female detective when she got scared by a toad and took a dive into the quarry garden."

When nobody greeted this theory enthusiastically, the colonel looked around with true Yahoo defiance.

"What's wrong with that?" he demanded. "Anybody got anything better to offer?"

Nobody had. Gail cast the G-2 man one look of scorn and then departed, Sue Anne trailing her.

"That nap idea doesn't sound a bit bad to me," Sir George Pakenham said, with a yawn. "If you people will excuse me . . ." He left, and Grafton and Ward tarried only long enough to remember their own sudden need for a siesta before they departed the *lanai*.

"And I," Barbara Grafton said, starting up from her lounge chair, "don't propose to waste another beautiful afternoon. I'm going to find Boyd and ask him if Creepy can run me over to St. George's in the outboard."

"And miss the grilling?" Terry James asked mockingly.

"You don't want to be there when the intrepid inspector unmasks the killer?"

"What killer?" North demanded. "It was an accident."

"Ah, but that's only what you think," Terry grinned. "Patricia was really thrown into the quarry garden because she wouldn't tell us where she had the plans for the new space missile hidden. You see, Yahoo, we're all Russian spies—they call Barbara here Bloodthirsty Babs in Moscow."

"Oh, Terry, for God's sake," Barbara said disgustedly, and stalked off in search of Boyd.

"Don't forget cocktails at five sharp, Barby," James called after her. He explained to North. "We're going to stoke up on drinks at five, then go see a Gombey dance over at the castle. We'll have a steak-out on the beach after the dance."

"Swell," Yahoo nodded, his eyes still on the slender yet voluptuous figure of Barbara James Winslow Grafton as his hostess walked away, her long legs and straight back detracting nothing from the soft appeal of her supple haunches.

When she was out of sight, Yahoo permitted himself a sigh and turned to Terry James. "That's quite a sister you have there, son," he told the playboy. "Grafton's a lucky feller."

Terry slouched in his chair, a tall, frosted glass in his hand. "She is something, isn't she?" he said softly. "And you're right, Grafton's lucky—too lucky. He doesn't deserve her."

"Well, now, I didn't say that," North told the younger man. "Your brother-in-law seems like an all-right *hombre* to me, even if he did sorta lose his temper with you in the garden this mornin'."

James grunted. "Hell, he couldn't hurt anybody; too soft. No, I'm not sore about that." He drained his glass and stood up. "What burns me up," he said, after a pause, "is that everybody talks about him being such a financial genius. Hell, if it wasn't for Barby's money, he'd be flat on his behind right now."

He caught himself and glanced sharply at Hugh.

"Forget I said that, will you?" he asked. "And if you're worried about Grafton not being able to carry his weight in the Paratina deal, don't be—Barbara's money will see him through."

"Sure," North nodded. "That was what I was figgerin', if you wanta know."

And his brain said: *Yes, Barbara's money will see Grafton through—if she'll let him have it.*

When James was gone, Hugh yawned and said in his Yahoo Gregory bellow: "Looks like the party's busted up, Kenny-boy. We might as well go back and have another crack at them figgers."

"Yes, sir," Trotter said obediently. He trailed his colonel out of the *lanai*, into the house, and down the hallway to their rooms. When they reached the doorway of their suite, Hugh silently indicated one of the markers they had set to announce intruders. It had been disturbed during their absence, nothing too unexpected.

North flung open the door, stopped on the threshold.

"Well, well, well," he boomed. "Just make yourself to home, son. Repayin' my visit to the boat, are you?"

Stan Gibbons sat in a high-backed chair facing the door. The ichthyologist-pornographer smiled gently at the G-2 colonel and nodded. "Didn't think you'd mind if I came in and waited for you," he said. "I've got something I'd like to talk over with you, Mr. Gregory."

"Why, sure," said the delighted colonel and half turned to Kenny Trotter. "Kenny-boy, s'pose you mix us up a coupla drinks, like a good feller."

Stan Gibbons' voice was suddenly made of frost-rimmed steel. "Kenny-boy," he grated, "s'pose you come in here with your hands up. You, too, Gregory. And be careful—right now I'd like nothing better than an excuse to let you both have it."

Quite magically, an evil-snouted automatic had appeared in Gibbons' hand; as swiftly, the ichthyologist's charming, handsome face had been covered by a mask of vicious fear and hate.

"Okay," he snarled. "Hand over that notebook you took off

my boat, you comic cowboy sonofabitch, before I splash your
guts all over the deck."

[4]

There was a second's frozen silence and then Hugh gave
voice. "Hey, what's wrong with you?" he cried. "Is this some
kind of a joke?"

Gibbons was motioning with the pistol. "Try any funny stuff
and you'll see what kind of a joke it is," he grated. "Get over
against the wall, you two. Trotter, close that door."

Kenny reached behind him carefully and brought the door
to. Then he moved over beside Hugh, his hands raised at
shoulder level.

"What is this, a stickup?" North demanded.

"You know what it is," Gibbons said bitterly. "I want that
notebook you got out of the bilge—the one with the red
cover."

"What's a bilge?" the colonel asked. The look of stupefied
amazement was intact on his artificially flushed face, his eyes
were popped, his uplifted hands trembled slightly, but the
G-2 officer was watching, dissecting Gibbons' every move,
estimating his next. If the ichthyologist-pornographer had
read the right books or seen the right movies he might tell
them both to turn around and lean against the wall at arm's
length, practically the only position which rendered a trained
man almost impotent in defense—oh, Gibbons could be over-
powered from that position but it would require a dangerous
maneuver, seeing that Kenny stood so close beside him.

"A bilge is what you broke into," Gibbons growled. "Your
damned snooping is going to make more trouble for you than
you ever knew existed, Gregory."

"You mean because I saw that sack of dirty pitchers you
got under the floor?" North asked. "Hell, man, I won't squeal
to Gail about you havin' them—if you'll let me keep the two I
just happened to let my fingers stick to."

"Shut up," the handsome man snarled. "Keep your hands

up, both of you. I'm going to find that notebook and I know it's on you somewhere, Gregory; it's not in this room."

He walked toward Hugh and the G-2 man grinned inwardly; Gibbons quite obviously had not read the right books nor seen the right pictures. The colonel waited, his muscles tensing beneath the ornate regalia of Yahoo Gregory. Gibbons came a step closer, another.

"I don't know what the hell this is all about," Hugh complained, "but I'm tellin' you, podner, that—"

And he exploded in a bombshell of furious action. One of Hugh's knees came up, a hand chopped down, the colonel's other hand caught Gibbons' left wrist and snapped it up back of the ichthyologist as Stan spun about, the automatic clattering to the floor.

"Ow!" Gibbons shrilled as North applied pressure. "Look out, damn you—you're breaking my arm!"

"Sorry, dear," the colonel grunted, and turned Gibbons about again, swung with a pile-driving right. The G-2 officer hated blackmailers only a little less than he did pornographers; the punch blasted Gibbons at the point of the younger man's chin, and Stan's head snapped back as he went toppling into a chair.

He was not quite knocked out; merely stunned past comprehension for a full minute. When he finally climbed out of his daze he found himself looking up into the eyes of a changed Yahoo Gregory.

"Okay, Gibbons," North said in a clipped voice—his real voice, "suppose you start talking."

Gibbons did not seem to notice the change in North. "You're the one who should talk," he managed. "You broke into my boat and stole my property."

"Your blackmail payoff list, you mean?" North rasped.

"Listen, I—"

"Shut up. Where did you get those cards?"

"Cards?" Gibbons asked, his eyes widening a trifle. "You mean those marked decks?"

"I mean a certain marked deck; the one with the notched

edges," Hugh growled. "Did you take them out of Patricia's room before or after you killed her?"

Stan Gibbons flung himself back in his chair, his face wrenched by terror, his mouth agape. "Murder?" he gasped. "I don't know what—I didn't murder anybody. I know you people play rough in your big deals but you can't frame me for a murder. So maybe I did pick up a few dollars with my pictures—that's all I did."

"Where did you get the cards, then?" North pressed on.

The man in the chair made ineffectual motions with his hands. "Hell, you can buy marked decks in the States," he said. "They have catalogues full of that stuff. But you can't use a queer deck in a regular house game—they'll spot you in a second. I keep those around for friendly games, bridge or rummy."

Hugh stared hard at the ichthyologist-photographer, doubt beginning to crowd into his mind. "You know damned well I'm not talking about those regular marked decks," he said after a pause. "I'm talking about the deck with the notched edges—Judy Forthier's deck."

Gibbons doggedly shook his head. "I don't know what you mean," he said, a touch of a whine in his voice. "I've got five or six packs of queer cards in that sack you took the notebook out of, but I don't know anything about Judy Forthier's cards. You mean Grafton's secretary who drowned, I suppose?"

"How many Judy Forthiers have you had around here?" Kenny Trotter asked acidly.

"Well, I hardly knew the girl," Gibbons protested. "Don't hang anything about Miss Forthier on me. She was Gail's friend, not mine." The handsome young man in the chair swiveled his eyes toward Hugh again. "Who are you, anyway?" he asked. "What's this all about? Are you police?"

"Never mind who we are," North rasped. "You're the one who's going to answer the questions for a while. Now, who are you working for?"

Gibbons' brown eyes seemed honestly puzzled. "Working for? I'm not working for anybody but Stan Gibbons—I never have."

"Don't give me that," the colonel barked and came a step closer to the man in the chair as Gibbons shrank faintly. "Let's hear some names of the people who are paying you, or do you want your face spoiled—permanently?"

Like most overly handsome men, Stan Gibbons' most vulnerable spot was his face. The ichthyologist-blackmailer threw up a forearm to cover the chiseled profile, the dimpled chin. "I tell you I don't know what you're talking about," he squealed. "If you're police, I want a lawyer."

"You'll need a lot of good lawyers before you get out of this jam, Gibbons," Hugh said in a level voice. "If you insist on protecting the people you're working for, a whole battery of lawyers won't do you any good—you'll hang."

"Hang? For what? I swear I don't know anything about any murder!" Gail Grafton's beloved cried. "I told you I shook down a couple of women with my pictures, I've dealt some queer cards in a couple of games—maybe I've taken a few bucks that didn't belong to me but it wasn't murder, for God's sake!"

"Who paid you to let them use your bilge hideaway to stash those cards, then?" the colonel demanded.

Again that stubborn headshake. "I keep telling you I don't know what you're talking about," Gibbons wailed. "When you said you'd been aboard the boat I thought I'd better check to see if you'd been snooping around the bilge. I didn't think there was a chance you had, but in my business you can't take chances."

"I can imagine not," North murmured.

"Yeah. So when I went through the stuff in the oilskin sack I saw the red notebook was missing. Maybe a couple of pictures, too—I didn't take the time to go over them all to make sure the file was complete. Anyway, I came back to shore and waited for you here. Then you came in and—well, you know the rest."

"Indeed we do," Kenny said brightly, "including you calling Mr. Gregory a comic cowboy sonofabitch."

"He's not Yahoo Gregory," Gibbons said sullenly. "I don't know who he is but—" He peered up at North, hope dawning in the brown eyes. "You asked me who I was working for—you must be working for somebody, yourself. Pakenham? Ward? What's your angle?" He hunched forward in his chair, licking his lips nervously. "Maybe we can settle this without anybody getting hurt."

"How would you suggest?" Hugh asked stonily.

"Well—well, maybe a few bucks can make you forget you ever went into that bilge," Stan Gibbons said. "Maybe you fellows can keep your mouths shut about my little business for the right price, eh?"

"Such as how much?" the colonel asked.

Gibbons glanced from Hugh to Kenny and back to the pseudo Yahoo Gregory. He licked his lips again. "You name it," he suggested.

"Ten thousand," North said.

Gibbons considered and then nodded slowly. "I can get it but not right away," he said. "Ten thousand? Sure, I can get that; I'd be willing to pay you boys that much to keep your lip buttoned."

"Aw, nuts, boss," Kenny put in, donning the new role easily, "this guy is talking through his hat. Where's he going to get ten grand when he's in hock for the dough he dropped at the tables?"

"I can get it! I can get it!" Gibbons cried. "Just give me— give me twenty-four hours to raise it. How's that? Just twenty-four hours."

"You can be a long way from here in twenty-four hours in that boat of yours," Hugh said.

"With Boyd watching? Don't be crazy. Besides, you can keep the notebook 'til I pay off. Fair enough, isn't it?"

"Who's going to give you ten thousand?"

Gibbons flung out a hand toward the main part of the house. "Man, you didn't look those negatives over very carefully, did you?" he asked North. "If you had you'd have seen a beauty, the prize of the lot. Torry James."

"Who hasn't got a dime of his own," Kenny said.

"But his sister has plenty," Gibbons argued. "She's been shelling out for James ever since he was old enough to get in trouble, and she'll pay again when I show her a print of Terry in the pose to end all poses."

"If that print's so good, how come you haven't cashed in on it before now?" North asked.

"Because I've been trying to marry Gail Grafton, that's why," Gibbons shot back. "Barbara's making it tough enough on me as it is, even knowing I've got something on Terry that will let me lower the boom if she gets too nasty." The handsome mouth curled in a cruel smile. "Besides," Stan added, "I enjoy seeing the beautiful bitch squirm, knowing I've got her brother by the short hair."

"But if you collect now," the G-2 colonel said, "you'll sell out your chances of getting Gail. Barbara may pay the ten thousand but you'll lose your hold over her, won't you?"

Gibbons shrugged. "So I get another heiress to work on," he sniffed. "Matter of fact, I've been thinking of pulling out on Gail, anyway. I've got the sneaking suspicion her father's close to broke."

Hugh North eyed the specimen in front of him with his loathing carefully held in check. He might despise Stan Gibbons with all his heart and he might have made up his mind long before that Gibbons would victimize no more women for a long, long time, but he had to admit one thing: Stan Gibbons was not the killer of Judy Forthier.

In fact, he was almost certain that Gibbons did not have any idea of what North had been talking about when he had asked the blackmailer about Judy Forthier's coded playing cards.

He sighed. Gibbons would have made such a satisfying man to be the villain of this piece. The G-2 colonel hoped that British law could provide a nice long prison sentence for a man who doped girls with aphrodisiacs and then photographed the helpless victims' crazed antics, but North was pretty sure that such a crime was not a capital offense. And Gibbons would have looked so good at the end of a rope.

He turned to Kenny Trotter and said: "Go hunt up Inspector Boyd, Lieutenant. I guess it's time we showed our hand to him, to make sure this louse gets what's coming to him."

From the doorway came a drawled: "No need to hunt me up, old boy. I'm right here, ready and waiting."

[5]

The inspector sauntered into the room, hands in his pockets, shoulders sagging with his ineffable weariness, his eyes reproachful as he looked at Hugh.

"Shouldn't have played games with us in that cowboy suit, y'know," he murmured. "Not legal, assuming another man's identity, even a freak's. I'm sure the laws provide a stiff penalty for such a thing."

Stan Gibbons clutched at straws. "They were trying to shake me down, Inspector," he cried. "They wanted ten thousand dollars—either I paid or they'd frame me for some murder."

"Now, really, this is too much," Boyd said sadly, his eyes still on North. "Impersonation and attempted extortion." He clucked his tongue.

"But he did!" Gibbons yelled. "They said—they said I could get it from Gail. They said—"

"Oh, I know most of what they said—and what you said," Boyd interrupted. "I was listening at the door, I regret to say. Hated to do it. Not at all commendable, eavesdropping, but they say my type of duty demands it on occasion." He half turned and called: "Oh, Constable."

Lunt, the young officer in the silver and gray uniform, appeared in the doorway. Boyd nodded negligently toward Stan Gibbons. "Take this unspeakable thing over to St. George's in the launch, will you, like a good chap?" His washed-out blue eyes moved back to North. "I take it you're finished with him for the time being?"

The colonel considered. "You can have him," he nodded. "I would appreciate it if you'd smuggle him off the island, though. There are a couple of people I don't want to know about this."

"Easily done," Boyd murmured. "So happens that they're

all gathered in the library waiting for me to come in and start machine-gunning questions. Haven't the slightest idea of what I'm going to ask 'em. Bad case of stage fright, I'm afraid. But it will be easy to get this clot off Plunder Island with a minimum of notice. Constable?"

As Stan Gibbons was being led out of the room in the grasp of the thin-mouthed Lunt, the ichthyologist-pornographer turned with a last desperate cry. "What's going on here?" he asked. "Who is this man claiming to be Yahoo Gregory, Inspector?"

"I have no doubt we'll find out all in due time," the languid man in the white linen suit smiled. "Now run along with the constable like a good chap and let the air you've fouled clear."

Gibbons was borne off, muttering incoherently, and Boyd turned back to North, smiled his faint smile, and strolled across the room to drop into a chair. He thrust his legs out in front of him, crossed his ankles, and asked conversationally: "Would you be good enough to tell me who you really are, both of you?"

Into the hesitation that greeted his remark, the Bermudian remarked: "I've known for the past ten minutes that you're not Yahoo Gregory—unless you're a remarkably healthy ghost."

"Ghost?" asked a puzzled G-2 colonel.

Boyd nodded. "Good thing you were ready to show your true colors," he said mildly. "Otherwise, there'd have been no end of work for me, I'm afraid. You see, I just got word from Hamilton via the patrol boat radio that the real Yahoo Gregory dropped dead in New York City."

For one of the very few times in his career, Hugh North found himself without a ready explanation.

"Oh, the real Yahoo was traveling under another name," the inspector went on, "but he was identified by things found on him, I'm afraid."

He snapped his fingers in an exaggerated gesture of sudden recollection. "Which reminds me," he went on. "One of my chaps—oh, I have half a dozen of 'em scattered around Freebooter's Hall now, y'know—happened to overhear a phone conversation a few minutes ago. It was a call for Mr. Gregory from Salt Lake City. Utah, I believe?"

The colonel nodded silently, waiting.

"A Mr. Van Huse asked the person who answered the telephone—Mrs. Grafton—to have Mr. Gregory call back immediately. It seems Mrs. Grafton was slightly confused; although you were here, she said you weren't available at the moment but she'd have you call Salt Lake City as soon as you came back from wherever you were supposed to be."

The inspector's smile flickered again. "I rather imagine it was somebody warning you that the genuine Mr. Gregory had yahhed his last hoo, don't you think?"

The G-2 colonel nodded. "Yes," he said pleasantly, "and I also suspect Mrs. Grafton thought the call concerned an entirely different matter, something that washed out her husband's big deal. She wouldn't want me to get that news if she could possibly help it—at least not until the Gregory money was paid into the pot."

"Oh, I shall want to hear all about the big deal," Boyd nodded. "But first, d'you mind telling me who you are?"

"My name's Hugh North, Colonel, Army Intelligence."

"Heard of you," Inspector Boyd sighed. He ducked his head toward Kenny. "And he's—?"

"Lieutenant Trotter, my aide," North supplied.

"How d'you do. And I'm Inspector Boyd of the Royal Bermuda Police, as you know. I don't suppose we need go through the business of showing our badges and all that, do you?"

North shook his head with a smile. Boyd seemed happy that this was going to be a friendly session. "Now if you'd oblige me by telling me just why you're here posing as Yahoo Gregory and his secretary, we can toddle along to that interrogation in the library," he said. "I suppose it's about the big deal?"

North nodded. "And Judy Forthier's death," he said.

"Miss Forthier's death?" Surprise. "It wasn't a plain drowning, then? Oh dear, and I so hoped that the Forthier case and this murder had no connection." His eyebrow quirked. "You know who Patricia really was, Colonel?"

"No. My guess was that she was Pakenham's agent on the scene."

"Quite right," Boyd nodded. "Fingerprints showed she was a lady with the unlovely name of Irma Gottleib, what I believe you Americans call an old pro in the adventuress game. C.I.D. found she'd done considerable undercover work for Pakenham from time to time. When Miss Forthier was drowned—or whatever you think became of her—Pakenham must have rushed her in here as Judy's sister."

He used his thumb to rub the tip of his nose thoughtfully. "Which may eliminate Pakenham as Patricia's murderer but which also brings up the question of whether he arranged Miss Forthier's death so Patricia could move in."

He eyed North quizzically. "Mind giving me your expert opinion of the quarry garden business?" he asked. "Did the killer actually think he'd get away with the broken neck cause of death? Didn't he think we have autopsies in Bermuda?"

"Not to sound enigmatic, Inspector," Hugh replied, "but I'd like a little time to wrap up some conclusions before I answer that, if you don't mind."

"Oh, not at all," Boyd said. He rubbed his nose again, sighed, and said: "Well, here I go being inquisitive again but I'll have to ask you about the big deal, y'know. My headquarters is understandably anxious to know just what's going on down here."

The G-2 colonel hesitated, then replied. "I'm afraid the details will have to wait on my headquarters' okay, but I can tell you this much: My government was working to prevent a revolution in a Central American country that might have put the Reds in the driver's seat down there. I can also add that the big deal is off, the revolution is off, the Commies will have to try something else."

"And Grafton was mixed up in this revolution? Ward and Pakenham, too?"

North nodded and felt called upon to add: "They just viewed the thing as an investment. I have no doubt that the thought of the Communists capitalizing on the revolution never entered their minds."

"I see," Boyd nodded. "And you came in here as Yahoo Gregory and worked with these chaps as another millionaire and never gave my government a hint as to who you were." He frowned faintly. "Y'know, my Foreign Office is apt to get quite snorty when they find out you Yanks have been climbing our fence again."

"And your C.I.D. has never climbed our fence?" Hugh asked softly.

Boyd gave his first genuine, wholehearted grin. "Perhaps," he said. "Perhaps not. If we have, we seem to have had better luck than to have our eccentric millionaires drop dead in the middle of things, in any case."

He leaned further back in his chair, folded his hands across his middle. "And now what about Judy Forthier?" he asked. "I'm dreadfully sorry I must ask you these things, but if we're going to work together you'll want me to know what you've done and what you're aiming at, won't you?"

"And if I don't tell you," Hugh returned, "what then?"

Boyd's face fell. "You disappoint me, Colonel. Of course you want me to work with you—you'll find it much more pleasant than being tootled over to St. George's, you and your aide, to try to continue the case from a cell next to Gibbons'."

Hugh did not lose his smile. "I expected as much," he said ruefully, "and of course it's your rightful due, to get the information we've managed to dig up. All right, here's the story of Judy Forthier and Patricia in a few words."

And the G-2 colonel told Inspector Boyd about the notched deck of cards, Patricia's words to him while they walked up from the pier, his visit to Patricia's rooms, the discovery of the missing cards aboard Gibbons' ketch, the shot that had narrowly missed killing him, Grafton's "suicide note." Boyd took it all in silently, never offering an interruption. When North was finished, the Bermudian asked:

"And do you know the killer, Colonel? Can we make an arrest?"

"Not yet," North said. "I've got it pretty well narrowed down but nowhere near enough to make an arrest. I'll need a little more time—possibly another day. That is, if you're willing to keep the news of Yahoo's death from reaching these people so I can have a free hand."

"Of course you may," Boyd sighed. "Tickled to death to let you do the work, to be honest about it." He got up from his chair, dabbed at his mustache, and asked: "Anything special you'd like me to do in this session that's coming up? What about Gibbons—keep his arrest quiet?"

"No," North said, "I'd like that to get out. Also, you might mention the filthy pictures, the crooked dice."

"Done," Boyd nodded. "How about the trip to Castle Island to see the Gombey dance—want me to put my foot down on that?"

"No," North said. "You might encourage it. Say Gibbons was arrested for pornography—no connection with Patricia's death. Just happened to stumble onto some of his wares while going over his boat. Also, you might ask them who visited the ketch in the past twelve hours or so—at any time since Patricia's death."

"I can tell you three who were aboard," Boyd offered. "Ward, Pakenham, and Grafton came back from Hidden Bay aboard the ketch when their boat broke down this morning. They hated to take Gibbons' offer of a lift, but they hated the idea of walking more. I'll ask 'em, though; there might have been some others slipping aboard, and one of them might have planted the Forthier cards in the bilge—I suppose that's what you're aiming at."

North nodded. "Not much hope of flushing our killer that way," he admitted, "but somebody might make a slip, eh?"

"That's what we build our careers on, Colonel," Boyd nodded. "Other people's slips. And luck. Just now, f'rinstance; I was coming to your rooms to ask you about how you could be Yahoo Gregory when Yahoo Gregory had just dropped dead in New York, and something told me to listen at your door before I knocked. I listened, I heard you and Gibbons have your chat, and look at all the work it saved me."

His face fell and he sighed. "Usually, though, my luck is the filthiest," he added. "It's bound to be in the session coming up now."

[6]

"I'll try not to keep you any longer than I have to," Inspector Boyd said as soon as he got silence in the library. "First, there's been an arrest made since I last talked to you."

"An arrest?" It was Wesley Grafton's hoarse voice. The millionaire's face was red and sweating as he stared at the inspector. "Who? Creepy again? I told you you were making a mistake—"

"No, not Creepy," Boyd interrupted, smiling. "We're convinced that Creepy—ah—got a bit excited and confessed to that ridiculous business of frightening the young lady into her fatal fall. Absolutely impossible, of course. No, we're still keeping an eye on Creepy but we're satisfied he's innocent of any worse wrongdoing than—er—misapplied loyalty."

"Loyalty?" Barbara Grafton asked sharply. "What do you mean? Loyalty to whom?"

"Perhaps Miss Gail can help us out there," Boyd suggested.

Gail Grafton's lovely eyes widened as she met the inspector's bland gaze. For a moment she flushed, then her cheeks returned to their normal admirable coloring. "So that's what happened," she said in a low voice. "Creepy saw me and—and when he found Patricia's body he thought *I* was involved and —oh, the dear, silly fool!"

"What is this?" Grafton demanded. "Gail, what are you talking about?"

The girl shot one glance at her stepmother and then faced her father, her chin up. "I guess Creepy saw me coming back from—from Stan's boat last night—this morning," she said. "You may as well know; I went back to Stan last night after I left you, when you thought I went to bed."

"Oh, Gail!" Grafton's exclamation was agonized. "After all you know about that skunk—the warnings you've had that the man's no good."

"I don't believe any of you," the girl retorted. "Just because Stan hasn't any money you all—you all tell lies about him."

Barbara Grafton's voice was cold, bitter. "Didn't I tell you it was useless to try to reason with her about Gibbons, Wesley?" she asked. "If the girl's determined to throw herself away on Gibbons, let her—maybe it's a case of *having* to, if she's been spending the night on his boat."

"Barbara!" Wesley Grafton swung toward his wife, his face wrenched with pain. "You can't say that—not even you! Not about Gail!"

Sir George Pakenham's voice crashed out. "Never mind about Gail and Stan Gibbons," the Britisher grated. "Who was it you arrested, Boyd?"

"Why, the chap that's causing all the uproar," the inspector replied. "Stanley Gibbons."

"You can't!" Gail shrilled, starting from her chair. "It's not right! He wasn't even here! Did my stepmother pay you to arrest him—is that it?"

Boyd's face lost its habitual pleasant expression for an instant. His mouth thinned and for a blazing moment his eyes came alive. "I'm sure you don't mean that," he said stiffly.

Gail's head dropped and a hand holding a handkerchief came up to her mouth. "I didn't," she sobbed. "But—but it's not fair! Why did you arrest Stan, of all people?"

"I'm sorry," the inspector said gently, "but I'm afraid the charges aren't very nice. The immediate count is possession of indecent photographs but there's suspicion of blackmail, too. We think he—er—used his pictures to extort money from those he snapped."

"Dirty pictures!" North exploded in Yahoo Gregory's voice. "Holy smoke!"

"Isn't that awful?" Sue Anne Pendleton cried. "And he looked like such a nice boy, too."

"He was anything but nice," Barbara said, her tone revolted. "Perhaps this will finally convince you, Gail."

Wesley Grafton's daughter seemed stunned. She sat with the handkerchief to her face, her shoulders bowed, her strong young body transfixed by the shock of Boyd's announcement. "I don't believe it," she said dully, after a long silence.

"Oh, it's quite true, I assure you," Boyd said. "Gibbons is

in Hamilton and they say he's practically confessed to the whole dirty business."

"You—it's a frameup, I tell you," Gail managed. "Stan just couldn't be that kind of person."

"I could have told you, kid," Terry James said, sympathy in his quiet voice. "I wish I had, now, before you got in so deep, but I thought you'd think I was butting in."

Pakenham's voice sounded again. "This is all very touching," he said, "but do you mean to say we've all been herded in here, penned up for nearly an hour, to wait for you to announce you've caught a common dirty-picture vendor? What does this man Gibbons mean to me, or to Ward, or even to Gregory?"

"Maybe nothing," the inspector admitted placatingly, "but I have to ask you some questions. Matter of form, really. First, who's been on Gibbons' ketch within the past twelve hours? Sir George, I know you and Mr. Ward and Mr. Grafton came back from your ill-fated fishing trip aboard the ketch. Mr. Gregory?"

"Uh-huh," North nodded. "I was aboard for a while just before I et lunch. I told everybody about it when I came back."

"Miss Grafton, you say you went back to Gibbons' boat after—"

"I won't listen, I won't listen!" Gail sobbed and sprang from her chair, ran out of the library weeping stormily.

Sue Anne Pendleton got up and spoke to Boyd over her rounded shoulder. "I wasn't on the boat at all, Inspector," she said. "I'm going out and take care of that poor child, if you don't mind."

She was gone after Gail before Boyd could tell her whether he minded or not. The inspector looked after the two women and sighed.

"All right," he went on after a pause, "was there anybody else? I'm asking this because we're fingerprinting the ketch. Might save embarrassment if you remembered being aboard her and spoke up now."

"This is ridiculous," Barbara Grafton sniffed (and Hugh

North, for one, had to agree with her silently). "We've all been aboard that damned boat at one time or another. Why, my fingerprints are probably all over the place. Does that mean I'm to be accused of being Gibbons' partner in blackmail or some such thing?"

"Er," said Boyd and seemed able to go no further.

"Well, I know you'll find my prints," Terry James offered. "I swam out to the ketch when it first got here this morning."

"Any special reason?" Boyd asked.

James shook his close-clipped head. "No, I was just swimming and I saw the ketch and—" He shrugged. "Maybe I thought Gibbons would buy me a drink—God knows he owes me plenty."

"You went to the ketch with no Owner Aboard flag up?" Sir George Pakenham asked coldly. "I noticed particularly that Gibbons took down the Owner Aboard flag when we came in."

"I don't know one flag from the other," Terry grinned.

"And you've been sailing all your life?" Pakenham murmured. "Odd."

There was a silence. North's brain told him: *Terry James was out there trying to find the picture Gibbons called the prize of the lot. Or—yes, possibly—planting Judy's cards.*

"What's all this mishmash about Gibbons' boat and who was on it?" Pakenham demanded. "What about that woman who broke her neck—what have you found out about her?"

"We've got her real name, for one thing," the inspector said. "Irma Gottleib. Familiar to anybody here?"

Without seeming to, Hugh North kept his eyes pinned on Pakenham, and the colonel had to marvel at the Britisher's total lack of reaction. The cold-eyed millionaire must know that his previous employment of Irma Gottleib as an undercover agent would be discovered sooner or later; he must have suspected, at least, that "Patricia" had not met her death accidentally, and yet there was not the slightest quiver or blink in Pakenham's response to indicate that this was anything but a name he had never heard before in his life.

Boyd waited as the people in the library shook their heads, one by one.

Wesley Grafton broke the silence. "Any idea why she came here, Inspector?"

"I'm sure I don't know if one of you doesn't," the man in the white suit replied enigmatically. "I hoped perhaps that one of you could give me a lead."

Pakenham got to his feet. "Well, it's obvious we can't," he said harshly, "and seeing that *I* can't, at least, will you kindly give me permission to leave here tonight? I'm due in Kenya the first of the month and—"

"Hey," Hugh North broke in, "how come you're pullin' out with the deal not signed?"

Pakenham threw the pseudo Yahoo Gregory a look of pure contempt before he turned back to the inspector. "Well, can I or can't I leave tonight?" he asked bluntly.

North turned his bewildered eyes toward Wesley Grafton. The master of Freebooter's Hall was staring woodenly at his shoes; he looked too beaten to raise his head at Pakenham's desertion. As North switched his puzzled stare to Townley Ward, the younger millionaire attempted a smile.

"We'll explain later, Yahoo," he said. "There's been a little difficulty but—well, there's something new on the fire."

Pakenham's laugh grated. "Difficulty? Just a hundred-million-dollar opportunity gone down the drain because we had a fool with us who insisted on mucking things up his own way."

Grafton's head came up at that and the millionaire's strained voice had both hate and despair in it. "Don't blame me for what happened, Pakenham," he cried. "How do we know you didn't talk to wreck the deal, yourself? You've been against it from the start—against it the way it was set up, I mean. You wanted to freeze me out before we even got started and—"

"Careful, Wes," Townley Ward warned. "Not here, old man."

Grafton glared at Pakenham for the space of ten seconds before his head sank again and he resumed staring at his feet.

The big, balding Englishman barked another humorless laugh and looked at Boyd again.

"Can I leave now?" he asked. "I want to get out of this madhouse."

The inspector was most apologetic. "I'm afraid not tonight, Sir George. There are a few things that need to be cleared up about—well, about several things. Why don't you plan on tomorrow morning, instead? I understand you're all going to Castle Island to see a Gombey dance tonight. You'll enjoy that, Sir George. You won't be bored, I'm sure."

6.

[1]

THERE WERE cocktails on the *lanai* that evening before the trip to Castle Island, with plenty of liquor, delicious hors d'oeuvres—everything but a semblance of a festive spirit.

Inspector Boyd took himself off after a Spartan drink and was seen no more, nor were any of his men, so the presence of the police could not be blamed for the general lack of gaiety.

"Probably peeping at us from the bushes," Barbara Grafton said as she sipped her drink, but Hugh knew this was not true. He had had a lengthy chat with Boyd after the session in the library and he knew where the inspector and his men had stationed themselves.

Gail Grafton attended the party, to Hugh's hidden surprise. The girl seemed to be making a valiant effort to fight her way out of heartbreak, but she did not appear to be winning any noticeable victory over her disillusionment. North watched the tall, lithe girl feign spurts of high spirits during which she talked too fast, laughed too loudly, was too frantic in her play at being bartender, and then relapse into tears, apart from the others, resisting Sue Anne's attempts to comfort her.

As for Gail's father, Wesley Grafton plied himself with

liquor in a determined, almost brutish, program of getting drunk. The G-2 colonel saw Townley Ward hovering about his friend anxiously, begging Grafton in undertones to take it easier, and saw the younger man rebuffed in surly fashion until Ward finally gave up.

Hugh North was back in his Yahoo Gregory role, although a bit more subdued than previously, still apparently concerned by Pakenham's words in the library. As Townley Ward passed, North grabbed his elbow.

"What goes on with the dook?" he asked loudly. "Why's he pullin' outta the deal?"

Ward looked around, replied in a lowered voice. "The Paratina deal fell through. Somebody talked and the government grabbed Guerra and shot him out of hand."

"Well, I'll be damned," North marveled. "You mean the whole thing's shot to hell?"

"Well—well, Wes has got some other lines out," Ward faltered. "I wouldn't be surprised but what he comes up with another idea as good if not better than the Paratina thing. Give him a while to sober up and get over his disappointment and he'll be right back in there, Yahoo. Who needs Pakenham? Hell, the three of us can—"

"Nothin' doin'," North said flatly. "I'm pullin' out, too. You boys don't play the kind of game I like. Two women dead and the police here and—what's people gonna think when they see my name mixed up with a goddam dirty-pitcher peddler, for God's sake? Nope, Ward, don't count on me to ante up any of my dough in any new scheme. I'm through."

"And I don't think I blame you," Barbara Grafton said, at North's elbow. The colonel turned to look down on a new Barbara. Where she had been cool, distant, now the mistress of Freebooter's Hall was flushed, her eyes wicked.

She got tight all of a sudden, North told himself. *Is she drinking fear as a chaser, perhaps?*

"I'm sorry, Barby," the colonel said aloud. "I'd sorta like to help your husband out but—"

"He doesn't deserve it," Barbara breathed, her eyes fixed on Grafton at the bar. "The promises he made me and now—now he'll probably come crawling to me begging me for more of my money. Well, he won't get it. He won't have me in as long as it takes to end this stupid marriage."

"You don't mean that, Barbara," Townley Ward said.

"I don't?" The woman's voice rang across the *lanai*, bringing all heads turning in her direction. "I'll show you how much I mean it, Townley Ward. As soon as Inspector Boyd lets me, I'm going over to Hamilton and see my solicitor—oh, not for a divorce—I can get that in Nevada—but to change everything that's in both our names back to mine. Luckily, I took the precautions of leaving strings attached. Otherwise, that fool would have thrown all my money away with his wild schemes that all go wrong."

"Now, Barby, old girl," Terry James cautioned, "let's not—"

"Yes, let her!" It was Gail Grafton, confronting her stepmother, her breasts heaving. "Let her say it so everybody can hear! She only married Daddy because she thought he had a few dollars more than her other husband; she's hated him ever since she found out he wouldn't sign it all over to her!" She thrust her face, still lovely despite her anger, toward Barbara. "Go get your divorce," she cried. "We'll help you—we'll do anything you ask, Daddy and I, to get rid of you. We'll—" She broke down, weeping, and Sue Anne put an arm around her shoulder to lead her away.

Barbara glared after her stepdaughter, her mouth crooked. "Very dramatic," she sneered. "I'd be more touched if I didn't know the daughter is as bad as the father."

"Come on, old girl," James said urgently, "you've had a touch too much. Suppose you pass up the Gombey dance and have a nap before the steak-out? I'll help you up—"

Barbara wrenched herself out of her brother's gentle grip. "Leave me alone," she said. "I'm all right. And I'm going to that Gombey dance if it's the last thing I do."

"Good show," Sir George Pakenham jeered. "On with the dance, eh?"

Hugh had noticed that Pakenham, his exit from Plunder Island denied, seemed to be taking his enforced stay philosophically with the aid of vast quantities of alcohol. Pakenham apparently had a capacity to go with his king-sized frame; he had been drinking steadily since the cocktail party started and showed no more effects than a slightly more contemptuous expression than was his normal air.

"Speakin' of the Gombey dance," North said, "how about gettin' started? I don't want to be so stinkin' I can't see what's goin' on."

"Good idea," Barbara said and started toward the pier. "Everybody who's for the Gombey dance, this way."

Gail Grafton did not even reply. North saw her father teeter over to her and bend over his daughter, but Gail shook her head firmly. The sodden millionaire appeared torn between his loyalties, wanting to stand with his daughter, hoping to save his marriage if he went with Barbara. Finally he shrugged with drunken gravity and moved after the wife who had just finished castigating him. Gail gazed after her father with deeply wounded eyes, then turned and walked slowly toward the big house.

Terry James and Pakenham followed Barbara and Grafton, and then Sue Anne tucked her hand in the crook of North's arm. "Come on," she whispered. "Barbara told me that if Gail didn't go tonight, Creepy would have the dancers do their real wild stuff. If Gail went, Creepy would have them do some little ole Sunday School dance. She's not coming so it looks like it'll be fun."

"And don't forget—we gotta date afterwards," North burbled. "You ain't gonna go back on what you said, are you?"

" 'Course not," Sue Anne breathed, and pressed her yielding bosom against North.

No one seemed to notice that Kenny Trotter, who had been with Hugh at the cocktail party, did not join the group wavering down toward the pier where *Amphitrite* waited. North silently approved of the way Kenny slipped away; the young aide was getting quite good at dropping out of sight without anybody's noticing.

Creepy was waiting at the landing, his face rigid, his eyes disapproving.

"Take us over, Creepy," Barbara said, flinging out an arm. "My last Gombey dance, Creepy, so make it a good one."

"Your last dance, Mrs. Grafton?"

"My very last. Tomorrow I'm going to leave this desert island and—"

"She doesn't mean it," Grafton broke in. He turned to the others. "Everybody get aboard," he cried. "All aboard for the Gombey dance."

"Where's Miss Gail?" Creepy demanded suddenly.

"She—she's not feeling well," Grafton said. "She won't be with us tonight. Everybody aboard."

Creepy seemed to North to want to say something else but whatever it was, the Pequot-Bermudian held his tongue. He gave orders to the boatmen who cast off the lines, and within a few minutes *Amphitrite* was foaming her way through the water bound for Castle Island.

The cruiser crossed the stretch of turbulence that marked the current of the Pass and then headed in toward Castle Island. To Hugh it looked as though Creepy was steering directly into a sheer wall of rock; the G-2 colonel peered into the gathering gloom until he saw a spur of rock made smooth by centuries of pounding waves, a natural pier which must be awash at high tide and which now jutted out two feet above the water. Creepy eased the cruiser up beside this platform, cut the engines, and leaped over the side to fix the bow and stern lines to ancient iron rings set in the rock wall.

"Heyo, Creepy?" a voice called out of the darkness. It was a hollow voice that echoed from some rocky confine.

"My God," Sue Anne squeaked. "Who's that, a ghost?"

"One of my men," Creepy said simply. "He guard de steps."

"What steps?" North asked. "I don't see no steps." He peered again and made them out, a steep flight of steps hewn out of solid rock, leading up through a narrow declivity in the cliff's surface.

"You expect me to climb that?" Sue Anne shrieked. "I'll die."

"I'm right with you, honey," North said. "I won't let you fall. C'mon."

With Sue Anne protesting that she just knew she was going to fall a million miles into the sea, Hugh helped the girl from Georgia up the steps. Barbara followed, Terry helping her when she refused Grafton's hand. Then came Pakenham, Grafton, Ward, and Creepy.

The steps were safe enough, wide and even-surfaced and lit after a fashion by‧the torches that suddenly bloomed up ahead of them. Above and ahead of the file of visitors from Freebooter's Hall, too, there thud-thudded a small drum, its hollow reverberations interspaced by a rhythmic, soft snarling sound and the shrill exciting notes of an off-key fife. To North, it was reminiscent of Haiti and Africa, where he had seen similar rites, some so sensational that even the cool-headed G-2 colonel could not remember them without a quickening of the pulses.

The party emerged from the tunneled steps, and North found himself in a hollow that lay at the base of the rugged watch tower. A bonfire at one end of the cleared space sent up leaping flames that illumined a segment of battlements which, forever torn at by the wind and battered by sea spray, had lost many sections of their original fabric.

Seated beside the fire were twenty or thirty natives, men and women in spotless white duck and gingham, their shadows cast on a parapet which the soldiers of England had trod many a weary hour of sentry go. Clasped between the knees of one man was a dance drum, what was called in Haiti a *papa* drum, while beside him another native used the palm of his hand to massage the *mama* drum, smaller and much higher in pitch. A third man held a snare drum from which he coaxed an insinuating muted tattoo.

"Sit! Wait!" It was an imperial command and for a moment Hugh had trouble identifying the speaker as Creepy. When the colonel turned, the Pequot-Bermudian was leaving, moving ghostlike to a place behind one of the ruined walls.

"When in Creepy's domain we do as Creepy says," Terry James managed with an uneasy laugh. "Take my advice and forget he's a boatman, Yahoo; now he's king of the Gombeys."

"Wait until you see him in his regalia," Ward half whispered, at North's elbow. "It's hard to believe it's the same Creepy. I've seen him dressed up as a Gombey priest several times and each time it was a shock when he appeared."

"Some of the Zuñi Indians can dress up pretty fancy," Hugh responded. "I remember the time—"

And stopped, because for all his experience in seeing natives in their ceremonial garb, the sight of Creepy emerging from behind the crumbling wall of the fort shocked the G-2 colonel speechless.

The erstwhile skipper of the *Amphitrite,* the rat-hunter, the dark-faced Quixote who had pointed the finger of murder guilt at himself to shield a girl he loved hopelessly from a great distance, John Cavendish, Creepy, was in all his primitive glory now. He wore a high, tubular headdress topped with crane feathers, and his head was wrapped in a gaudy cloth that also encircled his throat. He had exchanged his white, short-sleeved shirt for a multicolored, fringed cotton blouse and about his middle was a vivid sash. Creepy wore a skirtlike affair below the waist, a flaring garment fashioned of more wild-print cloth and decorated with brass rings, bells, tufts of horsehair, bunches of feathers similar to the wanga he had dropped in the quarry garden at Freebooter's Hall. His legs and feet were bare and about each ankle he wore a circlet of fur, attached to which were tiny bells.

Creepy carried an ancient cutlass in his hand, in all probability a relic of the British garrison of this fort and one which had been kept brightly polished through the years. Hugh North eyed the blade uncomfortably; its edge looked razor sharp, and if this dance produced the erotic-triggered hysteria he had seen at other native dances it could be a dangerous weapon.

At sight of their high priest, the other natives squatted about the fire set up a low, crooning chant. The drums beat more insistently, then rose to a savage crescendo as Creepy leapt into the center of the cleared space, brandishing his cutlass.

The Gombey leader began a dance, severely stylized and restrained in its first steps, but increasing its pace at the drums' urging until Creepy was a whirling dervish. With a final thump of the drums, the Pequot-Bermudian stopped stark still in the midst of a blurred spin, his cutlass upraised. The others set up a wail, hungry, demanding.

From behind another wall came a giant Negro clad only in a loincloth, a marvelous specimen of masculinity with massive shoulders and torso gleaming in the flickering firelight. He led a frightened goat kid, too terrified to bleat. At sight of the sacrifice, the natives set up a cry in some language their ancestors had brought with them from Africa or from the mountains where they had lived as Carib Indians.

The goat was brought to the center of the dancing ground, then tumbled to the ground as the giant grasped forehooves and hindhooves in his big hands. Creepy moved over the pinioned animal, his eyes bright, cruel yet ecstatic, and raised his cutlass. The blade winked in the firelight and fell.

There was a scream from the assembled Gombeys, a cry from Sue Anne. Beside him, Hugh could hear Barbara Grafton draw in her breath with a hiss. George Pakenham lost his cold reserve, grunted, and licked his lips. Townley Ward stared with a fascination that overcame revulsion.

When North looked at Creepy again he saw that the Gombey priest had been sprayed with blood by the kid's severed jugular. And deliberately, for now the boatman-turned-high-priest was smearing the dark fluid over his face and hands and legs, over every bit of him that was not cloaked by the gaudy costume.

The bloodletting served as a signal for the other natives to lose all restraint. There were gibbering cries as the men and women, so neatly clad in white duck and gingham a moment before, rent the trappings of civilization from their lithe bodies and leapt out onto the dance floor, clad only in brief batik-like skirts and loincloths of ocelot. Madly they plunged toward the dying kid, avidly they reached out to swab up the pumping blood and smear it over their own hard, muscular chests and soft, palpitating breasts.

All except the drummers; they stayed where they were, their hands busy pounding out a new rhythm, a thudding, urgent beat that held a sinuous, suggestive cadence. The fife, which had been silent since the party of whites had mounted to the plateau, now shrilled an eerie, spine-quivering challenge. Men and women, their nearly naked bodies daubed with blood, flung themselves into two lines, separated by sexes, and the dance began.

At the head of the two lines and between them, the high priest stood, his cutlass now a director's baton, pulsing out the rhythm of the beat. Each time Creepy's hand fell the two lines advanced a step closer to each other, the dancers jerking forward with a heave of their loins. Closer and closer they came, heads thrown back, eyes wide and staring as they grunted and squealed, until another half step would have put them in contact with each other. Then Creepy barked a harsh command and for an endless moment men and women strained there at their high priest's bidding, lusting for each other in a lascivious urgency that brought moans and cries - from men and women, their hips rotating, their pelvic gyrations less than two inches apart.

"Oh, my God," North heard somebody sob. It was Sue Anne.

Now the dancers were retreating, their hunger unsatisfied, their sex-thirst unslaked, until they faced each other from a distance of about fifteen feet. Another command from Creepy and the advance began again. Again it was halted within a tormenting hairsbreadth of completion.

"I can't stand it," Sue Anne muttered and Hugh felt her feverish hand in his, heard the Georgia girl's throaty voice in his ear. "Yahoo—please."

The G-2 colonel led the trembling girl out of the circle of onlookers, unnoticed by the others. He could have fired a cannon, he told himself, without breaking off the transfixed stares of the people from Freebooter's Hall. His last glance at the whites showed them all stripped of their guard; the man or woman didn't live who, having stayed past that first sacrificial slaughter, could tear himself or herself away from the sights revealed to his glazed eyes—except if he was a G-2 colonel or she was leaving for the purpose that was Sue Anne's.

Hugh North was nothing if not a self-disciplined man; his job called for the most rigid control over his own emotions at all times. Yet now he found himself stirred by the same primal compulsions that had so completely claimed the blonde from Georgia. Blindly, the two stumbled out of the firelight, away from the dancers, to a pitch black spot somewhere in the ruins of King's Castle and there Sue Anne turned to Hugh with demanding lips and hands and body.

"I don't care," she panted. "All bets are off now, anyway—I can do what I want."

North raised his mouth from the girl's neck. "Bets—what bets?" he asked.

"Never mind, never mind."

North fought with himself, managed to stave off the demands of his masculinity to ask: "What's goin' on, kitten? Level with me—why're you bein' nice to me instead of a young feller like James or Ward?"

"It's Barbara. She—oh, never mind."

"But I gotta know."

"Oh, for God's sake, stop talking. Can't you hear the drums? Didn't you see the dance? Are you made of stone?"

"Tell me first. What's the set-up between you and Barbara?"

The colonel's mind was stone cold now and Hugh's mouth twisted ironically in the darkness. This certainly was a switch. Usually, the beautiful temptress extorted information from her victim by withholding her charms until he talked; now it was the other way around. In any other circumstance, without the combination of too many drinks and that inflaming Gombey dance, Sue Anne Pendleton would have realized what was happening, but now the man-hunger that Wesley Grafton had mentioned was too piercing to be denied.

"Oh, I was supposed to make sure you and Ward came in with Grafton," Sue Anne gasped. "Barbara got me down here to sweeten you up if either of you got difficult. A girl will do almost anything if she's broke and wants the best things—

Barbara knew I'd do it—I've been doing it all my life, I guess. But now the deal's all off. I'm not working for Barbara or anybody else. I'm a woman! Oh, Yahoo!"

What would have happened then if there had been no interruption, Hugh North could only imagine later, but there was an interruption in the form of a sweeping flashlight's beam, the voice of Barbara Grafton.

"Sue Anne? Where are you? Sue Anne?"

With a groan of frustration, the girl from Georgia dropped her arms, whirled away from North, her hands fumbling at the disarranged bodice of her gown. "H-h-here," she managed. "Over here." And added savagely under her breath: "You bitch!"

Barbara came up to the couple, her voice slurred by drink and her roiled desires. "We're going back," she announced. "Nothing for civilized people to watch—even you. What've you two been talking about?"

"Talkin'?" North grinned. "Who wants to talk?"

"I suppose Sue Anne's been blabbing," Barbara said, and hiccoughed a laugh. "Well, it doesn't make any difference now. The party's over. Tomorrow I'm getting out of here for good. To hell with trying to get my money back—I'll write it off to experience."

With which she turned and teetered off, followed by Sue Anne and North. Back at the dance ground North found an ugly situation. Creepy stood facing Wesley Grafton, his dark face rigid with hate.

"You make me call de dance," the Pequot-Bermudian was protesting, "and then you stop it before she finished. My people don' like dis."

"To hell with your people," Grafton said drunkenly. "I tell you we're going back to the Hall. You can come back and finish this later if you have to."

"No," Creepy said with a sullen shake of his towering headdress. "Nobody can stop de dance and start it again."

He turned to the near-naked dancers standing by the fire, their bodies glistening with sweat, and barked a few unintelligible words. There was a savage growl in reply. Creepy waved the cutlass. "You all go," he cried in English. "You disobey me and you die of de sickness."

That broke the natives' rebellion. Muttering, whispering what North knew must be words of hate for these whites who had interfered, they turned to the scattered clothes they had ripped off and began climbing back into them.

"You go to de boat and wait," Creepy ordered the people from Freebooter's Hall.

It was a silent group that descended the rock steps. Now the liquor they had drunk sloshed dully in their bodies, boiled down to a wormwood residue by the turbulent emotions roused by the dance. There was no more deadening a weight than incompleted lust, and Hugh knew that the beach steak-out that had been planned to follow would need a great deal of liquor to rekindle any semblance of gaiety in this crowd.

He wondered what had happened at Freebooter's Hall during his absence, whether certain hoped-for developments had taken place, certain discoveries had been made to bolster his suspicions.

What he had now was this: Sue Anne Pendleton was Barbara's agent, a blue-blooded tramp brought here to seduce Yahoo Gregory and Townley Ward, if necessary, into going along with Wesley Grafton's Paratina plot. Ward had spotted Sue Anne's role immediately, as witness his coldness to the blonde at first meeting, so Sue Anne had concentrated on the man she believed to be Yahoo Gregory—doubtless on Barbara's orders.

But now Barbara had accepted defeat in her effort to get back at least some of the money Grafton had lost for her. But until tonight, Barbara had hoped to get that money back, had been willing to resort to acting as procuress to help Grafton's Paratina scheme—would she have gone the whole way for that money? Would she have wanted that money so badly that she would have murdered for it?

Judy Forthier had been killed because her work as a Counterintelligence agent had threatened to wreck the Paratina plot. Patricia had been killed because she was at least thought to have discovered Judy's murder and the killer's identity. Behind Judy's death was the motive, money; behind Patricia's, self-preservation.

Grafton was facing the grim specter of utter bankruptcy. He had invested a great deal of Barbara's fortune, so much that Barbara would stoop to peddling Sue Anne's flesh to try to get it back, via the Paratina deal. Grafton's heavy drinking was doubtless prompted by the hopeless picture, his financial collapse, the loss of his new wife, but was there something more? Did Grafton really believe that "suicide note" or was he in league with the killer who had written it—was he the killer himself?

Stan Gibbons—was he so easily dismissed as a murder suspect? Here was a man who made money from the foulest sort of blackmail, the doping of unsuspecting women with maddening aphrodisiacs in order to take pornographic pictures of them in their delirium. From the snapshots and negatives North had seen, it was obvious that Gibbons had used infrared film with filters and safelight boxes which would hide all hint of the exploding flashbulbs from his victims. A nasty business, Hugh told himself sourly, that no human would resort to except one with a perverted mind and a need for money.

But would Gibbons murder, out of fear or money hunger? If he had not killed "Patricia," how had he gotten those cards? Might Gibbons not have entrapped little Judy Forthier in his web and, confronted by her threat to expose him, have killed the Counterintelligence agent out of hand in a burst of panic? And then killed "Patricia" when she had found out what he had done? Gibbons had been within striking distance when "Patricia" was murdered; Hidden Bay was only a couple of miles overland from Freebooter's Hall.

And there was always Wesley Grafton, the man who figured to suffer most from Judy's exposure of the Paratina plot. And Terry James, who loved his sister so deeply—and her money that bought him out of scrapes; could he have killed Judy to protect Barbara's chances at sharing in the Paratina payoff?

Sue Anne Pendleton could not be forgotten in the list of suspects, in "Patricia's" case, at least. She had admitted that

she had hired out to Barbara; could she have been in somebody else's pay, as well—somebody who needed an "empty-
headed blonde" to get close to the suspicious 'Patricia" and
murder her, if need be?

What about Gail Grafton? She despised Barbara. Gail
would laugh at any money losses suffered by her stepmother,
certainly, but her father's losses by collapse of the Paratina
plot would be another matter.

Some of North's theories were admittedly farfetched, others
impossible on their face, considering the facts at hand. Yet,
as was his manner, Hugh North went over all the possibilities
as he descended the rock steps that plunged downward
through the narrow declivity in the face of the old fort's cliff.

At the rock landing, he surveyed the others as they boarded
the cruiser and headed for the bar in the cabin. *Drink up*, he
said silently. *With that dance on top of everything else, one
of you must be on the verge of losing your grip. Maybe
enough liquor will nudge you over the edge.*

[2]

Immediately upon the boat's return to Freebooter's Hall,
North hurried to his rooms ("Gotta see a man about a dog,
as the feller sez") and found Kenny Trotter waiting.

"Not too much, *mon colonel*," the young lieutenant said
ruefully. "Boyd's men checked out the ballistics on that slug
that nearly got you on the ketch. It was fired by Creepy's
rifle, all right, but that doesn't mean much. The .22 is kept
in a utility room off the kitchen; everybody knows it's there.
We went through everybody's room except Gail's—she was in
there, crying over Stan Gibbons. Didn't find a thing in the
other rooms."

"Nobody tried to get on the ketch, I take it?" North asked.

Trotter shook his head. "Nobody went anywhere near it.
Of course only Gail was here to try, unless one of the servants
is mixed up in this mess, and as I told you, she didn't move
out of her room. What luck at the Gombey dance?"

"All I learned was that Sue Anne Pendleton was imported to keep me happy in case I needed sweetening up to go along with Grafton's scheme. Barbara hired her for the job."

"Barbara?" Trotter's eyebrows shot up. "Surprising, don't you think?"

"Nothing about any of this crowd would surprise me much," Hugh said. "Has Boyd heard from Hamilton whether Gibbons has opened up any further?"

"Our Stanley isn't talking, except to holler for a lawyer. Understand he's having trouble finding somebody to take his case." Trotter lit a cigarette, blew smoke across the room in a long ribbon. "One thing we haven't paid much attention to, boss—the murder weapon. How come we haven't turned Free-booter's Hall upside down looking for the weapon and the fingerprints that must be on it?"

"We'd have to do just that, turn this place upside down and shake it hard," the G-2 colonel explained. "Even then it's twenty-to-one we wouldn't find it. Nothing easier to hide than a stiletto blade with its hilt off, or a sharpened steel knitting needle, or an overlong icepick that can be sitting in a kitchen drawer right now. As for fingerprints, our killer isn't the type to leave 'em."

"A sharpened knitting needle is easy to hide?" Trotter asked incredulously. "A stiletto blade is something you can just slip in your pocket and walk around with?"

"It's a cinch to hide something as narrow as either a stiletto blade or a sharpened knitting needle," North said firmly. "I remember a case where a stiletto blade was kept in a hol-lowed-out candle, smack in the center of a candelabra with everybody looking at it. No, Kenny, finding the weapon's a pretty hopeless job with the time we have. Our best bet is to locate it in the hand of the killer."

"Fat chance," Kenny gloomed.

"Oh, I don't know," North said philosophically. "If my hunch proves out, the killer may have to move again, and soon. Now, let's go to that steak-out. I'm hungry."

"You want me to taste your steak before you eat it?" the

colonel's aide asked. "In case the killer has pulled a switch from stilettos to cyanide?"

The steak-out was held on a beach to the north of Freebooter's Hall, a stretch of pure white sand on which Grafton's servants had set up a trestle table, beach chairs, tall torches stuck in the sand, and, of course, the ever-present bar. Working at the charcoal fire were two cooks in chef's caps. Maids carried the side dishes that went with the main course from a second fire over which was stretched a grill where warming plates rested.

Nobody except Hugh, Kenny, and Terry James seemed the least bit interested in food. Gail Grafton put in an appearance and tried hard to hide her heartbreak, but it was obvious that she had no appetite. Instead of paying any attention to the cooks' request for orders, rare or medium rare, the others clustered at the bar and resumed the business of trying to recapture whatever glow they might have had before the Gombey dance.

"You'd better go ahead and eat," Terry James advised. "When they get going at those bottles they forget all about food, and tonight it looks as though they've got their drinking shoes on, even Barby."

"Me, I'll give my likker glands a rest," Hugh said. "I gotta fortify myself for more drinkin' later on." He gave his order and Kenny chimed in with a similar request, medium rare.

Gail Grafton drifted across to the table and slipped into a place beside North. "What did you think of the Gombey dance?" she asked. "Sorry I—I didn't feel up to going."

"It's a good thing you didn't," the G-2 colonel replied. "Pretty rough for a young gal like you. Even got too raw for your daddy; he told 'em to quit when they were about halfway through."

"I heard he did," Gail said. "The dances I've seen weren't that kind at all—Creepy wouldn't let me see anything that bad, I guess." She summoned a faint smile. "Dear old Creepy—can you imagine him doing a thing like that to protect my good name?" And added bitterly: "My not-so-good name now, I suppose."

"Look, Miss Gail," Hugh said, "you don't want to let this throw you, this thing about Gibbons. Hell, you ain't the first gal that's been fooled by a no-good. What you gotta do now is forget all about him."

"I know," Gail said in a low voice. "It's easier to say than do, though."

"I know that, too," Hugh nodded. "But a young gal like you can do it—hell, it ain't the end of the world."

Gail glanced over toward the bar where her father was huddled beside Barbara, talking earnestly while the dark-haired beauty, obviously more than half drunk now, shook her head with heartless insistency. The girl beside North sighed, turned back.

"Daddy's the one I'm sorry for," she said, her voice muted. "I've broken his heart. His business deal has fallen through. Barbara's leaving him." Her deep eyes sought North's. "I don't suppose—no, of course not."

"You don't suppose what, Miss Gail?"

"You won't—well, sort of stick with my father, will you, Mr. Gregory—Yahoo?" Gail asked. "He needs a friend now as he never did before. Townley's not going to help him and Pakenham—well, you know Sir George. If somebody would just show faith in Daddy, stay with him long enough for him to recover from this Paratina thing—but I suppose that's asking too much from a comparative stranger when friends like Townley won't do it."

North twisted uneasily on the bench. "I'd like to, Miss Gail," he said uncomfortably, "but business is business. The Paratina deal looked like a good thing and that blew up in my face. Seems to me—well, you gotta admit I'd have reason to think a long time before I'd put any money into anything else your father set up, if this one came apart so fast."

Gail was looking down at her blunt-fingered hands, twisting on the tabletop in front of her. "I know," she acknowledged. "Maybe it's for the best. Maybe if Daddy has to—to get rid of all the things that have been cluttering up our lives, he'll feel better. I *know* Barbara's leaving him will help, even though Daddy may be a long time getting over it. But if we could get back to what we were once, happy people in happy surroundings, I wouldn't care how little money we had."

The steaks arrived then and Gail left Hugh. North spared the departing girl a long glance before he attacked his food, which proved to be delicious. Hugh and Kenny busied themselves devouring a tremendous meal while the people at the bar continued to sop it up, their voices rising with each drink. Gail wandered off alone and did not rejoin the group until the tipplers finally called a recess and wavered their way to the table.

It was Barbara Grafton who seemed to have been hit the hardest by her drinking. She sat down at the table on the opposite side from Hugh, and as North studied her he saw that her eyes were glassy, her head seemed heavy on her neck. Several times the patrician beauty seemed about to let her head loll down on her chest, but she caught herself each time and straightened with an effort.

She had brought a glass with her to the table, half filled with a mixture so dark that Hugh decided it must be seven-eighths whiskey. As Hugh watched, Barbara looked up and down the table, her face loose and uncertain in her drunkenness, and then raised her drink.

"Here's to the great state of Paratina!" she cried suddenly. And added: "God damn it to eternal hell."

Grafton, further down the table, turned his drink-bloated face toward his wife. "Please," he muttered. "Can't you take the bad with the good—why keep harping on it?"

"Good, what good?" Barbara demanded. "What have you ever done for me that was good? Spend my money, make promises you knew you couldn't keep—you call that good?"

Sue Anne Pendleton left her place and came up behind the drunken woman. "Come on, honey," she coaxed. "Let me get you back to your room for a little ole nap, what do you say?"

"Get away from me, you—you floozie!" Barbara blurted. "S'pose I tell everybody why I invited you down here, huh? S'pose I told 'em just what you are, a—"

Sue Anne's hand flashed around and the slap echoed over the stunned gathering.

"Don't call me names!" the girl from Georgia cried. "Don't tell lies about me, Barbara James, or I'll make you wish you hadn't. You're a fine one to talk! At least I do what I'm paid for—I don't climb out of one bed and into another because one man's got a dollar more than the other."

"Why, you—" Barbara lurched to her feet and dove at Sue Anne, but Wesley Grafton was there to bar her way.

The master of Freebooter's Hall managed some semblance of sobriety as he stifled Barbara's struggling. "Disgraceful," Grafton said hoarsely. "Barbara, you're drunk! Go to your room!"

"Make me," his wife spat. She was not lovely now, her hair straggling down over her drink-raddled face. "Make me, you —you sweaty pig. God, will I be glad to get away from you! Take the money I loaned you—call it a gift—only let me get away from you!"

She wrenched herself out of Grafton's grasp and staggered across the sand for half a dozen paces before she pitched forward and lay still. Wesley Grafton uttered a hoarse cry and ran to her side, knelt on the sand to turn his wife over.

"Only passed out, thank God," he said, a moment later. "Somebody give me a hand to carry her up to her room."

"Oh, I'll take her up, Daddy," Gail Grafton said, her young voice charged with a strange mixture of sympathy and contempt for the helpless woman at her feet. "I've done it before, you know."

Grafton protested but while he spluttered, Gail Grafton stooped, picked up the lifeless bundle that was Barbara Grafton, and carried her in her arms, as easily as though Barbara were a child.

And that, my sweet, does it! Colonel Hugh North told himself sadly.

[3]

Somewhere in Freebooter's Hall, a clock chimed three. The room in which Hugh North crouched was almost pitch black; there was a faint light at the curtained window, but it did little to relieve the darkness. From the bed came the stertorous breathing of the drunken woman, a semi-snoring that had kept up steadily since the G-2 colonel had slipped in through the window.

Perhaps she's smarter than I give her credit for, Hugh told himself. *Maybe she's even pegged me for a phoney Yahoo Gregory. But she's almost got to act tonight. Tomorrow, Barbara may be gone and with her all that lovely, lovely money.*

Barbara, North reflected, had helped immensely by getting so plastered—what better shape to be in for a reckless swim to "clear her head." Even better than the Judy Forthier story. Or perhaps the killer had another suicide note ready, although what reason could Barbara give for taking her own life—her lost love for Wesley Grafton?

It was getting late. The house had quieted down after Wesley Grafton had been put to bed by Townley Ward, burbling drunken incoherencies, in his own room, across the dressing room from this chamber. That was some time after "Yahoo Gregory" had announced that he had had enough, come along Kenny-boy, and had gone to his rooms, there to shed the hated Gregory costume and outfit himself in an all-black, close-fitting outfit that rather resembled a frogman's apparel, the ideal garb for invisible night travel. North had waited only to change his clothes before he had eeled down the length of Freebooter's Hall to Barbara Grafton's window. The "can opener" had done its work, and the G-2 colonel had taken up his position at least ten minutes before he heard Ward bring Grafton to his room.

North had expected the drunken millionaire to look in on his wife, but Grafton apparently had taken too much aboard to even do that. There had been sounds of the spurned husband fumbling about his room, then silence which gave way to loud snoring. The minutes had passed, the silence had deepened, and now it was three o'clock without a sign by the killer North expected to make her move—Gail Grafton.

It figured almost from the start, Hugh told himself. *The person who killed Judy Forthier had money as the only motive. Judy threatened the Paratina deal; Judy had to die.*

Judy was a Counterintelligence agent and she couldn't have been a fool; she must have kept her eye on the obvious enemies who might want her dead. Yet she let herself be backed into a corner and then was murdered, and by somebody she didn't suspect until the last second.

Now, who were our suspects? Grafton, Ward, Barbara Grafton, Creepy. If we hold to the money motive, we scratch Creepy, unless he was acting for somebody else and Creepy's whole make-up minimizes that possibility. Grafton? Possibly, but wouldn't Judy have guarded herself better against him? Would Grafton have offered that phoney suicide note if he had been the killer?

And besides, the one who killed Patricia, or whatever her name really was, was a woman, eliminating Grafton. That stab wound in the breast didn't cut the nightdress or robe. Patricia was nude when she was killed and that indicates her killer was a woman and a woman who had gained Patricia's confidence, as she had gained Judy's. Patricia was expecting me at three o'clock and she would have let me in but would she have let in another man except Pakenham, her boss? No. Pakenham wasn't on Plunder Island when Patricia was killed. It was a woman who killed Patricia and that woman killed Pakenham's agent because she thought Patricia was getting close, at least, to finding out who had killed Judy.

And perhaps Patricia was getting close. Perhaps Irma Gottleib knew the old card-edge code. Certainly Gail didn't place any significance in the cards until she must have spied them on Patricia and seen her working with them. Then she knew—or strongly suspected—that Judy had left a message on the cards, so she substituted another deck with meaningless marks on the side and switched decks. She didn't know the significance of the key letter, though—perhaps Irma, or Pa-tricia, didn't either—and she left that.

She cached the cards in Gibbons' bilge hideaway, and when she saw me board the ketch she took a shot at me with Creepy's rifle. Some little actress—she never turned a hair when I showed up hale and hearty; I wonder how she's tried to explain my not squawking about somebody shooting at me?

But to get back to the main thesis; it had to be a woman who killed "Patricia" and therefore Judy. That put Gail and Barbara on the spot. And possibly Sue Anne, but I never seri-ously considered Sue Anne; she's not physically strong enough.

So it was Barbara or Gail and—

The G-2 man left off his thoughts as the door to the bed-room door swung open silently.

Gail Grafton crept across the carpeted floor to the side of the bed. For a second she gazed down on the sleeping woman, and Hugh caught the fleeting glimpse of the girl's teeth as they showed in a hideous smile.

Then Gail's hand came around from behind her back and the G-2 colonel saw the dull gleam of metal. Gail crouched over the motionless form of her stepmother and brought the blade closer, closer, to the sodden woman's breast.

Hugh moved with whirlwind speed, yet when he reached for Gail's wrist it was with a judgment of distance that gave the girl no chance to lurch forward with that deadly blade in one last hateful stab. Gail found her striking arm—so lithe, so strong—caught in a vise and Wesley Grafton's daughter screamed, high and shrilly, like a wounded animal.

She turned on North then, spitting and clawing, her curses foul, her furious strength equal to a good many of the men with whom Colonel Hugh North had grappled in the course of his career. The girl's knee came up and North went side-ways to avoid the crippling kick; Gail's hooked left hand reached for the colonel's eyes, and Hugh was hard put to it for a second to escape the blinding slash.

And all the time he held the knife hand, held it up and away from him against every straining muscle that Gail Graf-ton could exert to bring it down. He was bending the arm

back, feeling Gail's mad strength flow out of her as her hope-
lessness swamped her, when the door burst open and Kenny,
Inspector Boyd, and the others rushed in.

7.

HUGH NORTH and Kenny Trotter were winging their way
back to Idlewild Airport in Wildcat Bill Allenby's fabulous
airplane later that day, a long, mild Scotch and soda, no bourbon and branchwater, in the colonel's hand.

North still wore the regalia of Yahoo Gregory for the reason
that the wardrobe he had taken to Plunder Island included
nothing more conservative, except the black skin-tight night
travel outfit which he did not consider exactly *de rigueur* for
the homebound flight. "But once I get back in civilization," he
promised Kenny, "nobody will ever get me into a pair of cowboy boots or a ten-gallon hat without calfroping me first."

"Back to civilization!" Trotter exclaimed. "You mean you
don't consider all that high living civilized?"

"Not my brand of civilized," North said firmly. "A more un-
civilized bunch of people I don't think I've ever met. Except
Creepy. He operated according to rules I could understand,
simple loyalty, undemanding love. And he was supposed to be
the savage among them.

"Poor Creepy," he added sympathetically.

"He sure was all broken up about Gail," Trotter nodded.
"Do you think he knew Gail was the killer?"

North shrugged. "I don't think he admitted it to himself,
even if he did. Like Wesley Grafton; he suspected Gail of killing Judy but he seized on everything, including that suicide
note, to try to prove to himself that she didn't."

Kenny sighed and sipped at his own drink. "It's still pretty
hard for me to believe," he admitted. "Gail Grafton seemed
to be the most normal one of the bunch, at first."

"Yes, but she really was the most vicious of the lot, even worse than her lover, Gibbons. You heard her when she made her confession; it was sweet Gail who set up her friends for Gibbons to dope and photograph."

"Nice kid," Kenny said grimly.

"Well, she was absolutely gone on Gibbons; she couldn't think straight where he was concerned."

"So she tried to pin everything on him by planting Judy's code cards in his little bilge cache," Kenny said cynically.

"No, she didn't intend to involve him," North corrected. "She just thought that was the safest place possible for those cards until she could get a chance to study them, find out what they meant."

"If Gail was so clever in her crimes, how come she dumped Patricia's body in the quarry garden? She must have known an autopsy would show the breast wound."

"You weren't there when she explained? I had it doped out before she verified what I thought. She was carrying Patricia —I'll always think of her as Patricia, not Irma Gottleib—to the Pass when Creepy crossed her path. You remember the quarry garden is south of the house, on the path to the Pass. When she heard Creepy, Gail had to dump the body into the quarry garden. It was just bad luck that the fall broke the dead girl's neck."

"And Creepy saw Gail and planted the wanga."

"He caught a glimpse of her after she ditched the body. Later, when he found the body—well, you know what he did then."

"What did Gail say about killing Patricia? Remember, I was busy filing a report to headquarters during most of that confession, *mon colonel*."

"She said that after Patricia left me—"

"I hate to break in, but just why did Patricia tell you she suspected Judy, her so-called sister, was murdered? What was her angle?"

"She was working for Pakenham and Pakenham wanted me scared out of the Paratina deal. Pakenham knew that if I pulled out, Grafton wouldn't have the necessary dough and could be frozen out, too. That would leave him and Townley Ward to whack up the investment between them—if he didn't get Ward out of it, too, somehow. Patricia did know there was something wrong with Judy's death—she may even have read the coded cards and gone on from there. She was probably prepared to give me a real song and dance, enough to scare me right off Plunder Island.

"Anyway, after Patricia left me, Gail went to Patricia's room and sat around and chatted awhile, waiting for the others to settle down. Patricia went to take her shower and Gail stabbed her there. Very convenient, the running shower washed the bloodstains away, what few stains there were. Then Gail took the time to substitute those cards, dress Patricia in robe and nightgown, and take her down the path toward the Pass. Creepy interfered and—but I told you about that."

"Judy got the same treatment except she went all the way to the Pass?"

"Yes. Gail says her father found out Judy was an undercover agent—the Forthier girl made a bad slip and Grafton caught her red-handed. Grafton blew up, even threatened to have one of those accidents happen to her, to save his deal. I doubt he would have gone through with it—he actually was fond of Judy—but he told Gail about it and she took over from there on her own hook. She says now that Judy didn't suspect her until the last minute. Gail stabbed Judy, dumped her body in the Pass, wrote the suicide note to give her father something to hang onto.

"Grafton was almost sure his daughter killed Judy but he did what she thought he'd do; he clung to the suicide note. When he told me about it, he came up with the pregnancy lie and named Gibbons just out of his hate for the man. But at the edge of the quarry garden, when he looked down at Patricia's body, he muttered: 'Why *her?*' That showed me Grafton knew Judy had been killed. It also indicated that Grafton knew the killer and was shocked to find that the killer had struck again."

Trotter finished his drink, moved to replenish it.

"When was it that you were sure it was Gail?" he asked his colonel.

"When Barbara announced she was pulling out," North replied. "You see, both Barbara and Gail had the same motive, in varying degrees. Barbara loves money and she was furious about Grafton losing some of hers; she wanted it back. The Paratina deal offered her husband a chance to recoup and pay her back—she wanted that deal to go through at all costs. Same thing with Gail; she knew her father was through if the Paratina deal collapsed, and she'd be willing to go to any lengths to keep it from collapsing.

"But then when the Paratina deal *did* collapse, Barbara wrote it off and announced she was pulling out. Which posed the big difference between Barbara and Gail; Barbara could continue to live it up with the money she had, even with what Grafton had taken from her—Gail couldn't. Gail was as broke as her father."

Hugh North paused and added significantly: "Unless Barbara James Grafton was drowned *before* she could change her affairs to shut Wesley Grafton out in the cold. I was banking on Gail having to move that night lest Boyd permit Barbara to go to Hamilton the next day and see her lawyer.

"Then, at the cocktail party before we went to Castle Island, Gail recovered from her quote heartbreak unquote over Stan Gibbons in curious fits and starts, just long enough to act as bartender every once in a while—especially when Barbara needed a refill. Gail spiked Barbara's first drinks, knowing that her stepmother was a curious type of alcoholic who, once she got off to a fast start like that, continued until completely stoned. You'll remember that when Gail carried Barbara off from the steak-out—and proved she was fully capable of carrying a big girl like Irma Gottleib down to the quarry garden, no mean feat—she said she'd done it before. She knew Barbara's drinking pattern; she had to make sure her stepmother got well plastered that night."

Kenny Trotter added ice tò his drink and started back toward his chair.

"There's one thing, *mon colonel*," he said. "Suppose you'd

crouched in Barbara's bedroom all night and Gail hadn't
shown up? Suppose Gail had decided to gamble against Barbara getting to her lawyer the next day? Suppose nothing had
happened?"

"She was almost sure to move fast," North said. "She
couldn't get Barbara plastered again before Barbara moved
out and if she wasn't drunk, Barbara wouldn't have let Gail
come within ten feet of her. It was a pretty sure thing that
last night was the night."

The G-2 colonel drained his Scotch and soda. "Besides,
podner," he bellowed, "what're you doin', doubtin' my infalli-
bility with such crazy questions? Ain't it enough that Gail did
show up and do just what I was dependin' on her doin',
Kenny-boy?"

www.ingramcontent.com/pod-product-compliance
Lightning Source LLC
Chambersburg PA
CBHW020638180626
46816CB00003B/1030